"It'll be lo-o-onely this Christmas, without you to lu-urve…"

I put my hands over my ears. "If you sing that song one more time…!"

Will threw back his head and howled again, "So lo-o-onely."

"Will…" Rosie said warningly, as she braked to avoid a man dragging a Christmas tree across the road. "Leave your sister alone, she's had a bad day."

Will went quiet for a few moments. Then he leaned forward, placed his face between the front seats of the car and began to croon in my ear, "So lo-o-onely…" I lashed out wildly with my arm and he ducked out of the way, laughing.

"Cut it out, Will, Emma's not in the mood."

"I *know that*, Rosie. I live in the same house as her, remember? The house that yesterday was so full of happiness and today is full of—"

"If you say another word I swear this is coming down on your head," I snapped, pointing at my school bag, which looked impressively heavy.

Will snorted but sank into silence.

I stared out of the car window. The rain streamed down the glass. This morning someone had put a Santa hat at a perky angle on the angel statue in Mrs Stevenson's garden. It was now drooping over one eye and the angel looked forlorn and depressed. I knew just how she felt.

Will opened his mouth again, then caught Rosie's eye in the rear-view mirror and shut it.

I didn't know what was worse: going on your very first date with Sam Harrison, the best-looking boy in school who was in the year above … and then being dumped by text *the same night*, or having a twin brother who teased you mercilessly *and* who was so popular that every girl in school wanted to go out with him. I was relieved when we pulled up outside our house.

"Thanks for the lift, Rosie," said Will, as he leaped out of the car. "See you in a couple of weeks." He dashed towards the front door, balancing his backpack on his head to keep his precious hair dry.

Rosie turned to look at me. "Why don't you wait a minute or two for this rain to ease up? Hardly Christmas weather, is it?" She scanned my face and frowned. "Are you OK?"

I shook my head. "Not really. School was awful – everywhere I went people were either giving me sympathetic looks or hurrying past me whispering gleefully."

Rosie smiled. "I know it seems bad at the moment, and I totally understand how disappointed you must feel, but it's not like you really *knew* this boy, is it? From what you've told me, the only thing you knew about him was that he liked football. You hadn't really had any in-depth conversations."

"Who cares about in-depth conversations?" I gasped. "He's the fittest boy in school! Everyone wants to go out with him. I'd been hoping he'd notice me for ages. I even pretended I was interested in football."

"But you're *not*."

"Exactly! But when he overheard me talking about it *really loudly* at the Christmas Fair, it got his attention, didn't it? He asked me out."

Rosie leaned over and pulled a lock of my long

dark hair. "Piece of advice for you. It's always best just to be yourself with boys, Emma, no pretending. And look at you – there's so much to like. I'm sure this Sam liked lots of other things about you as well as thinking you liked football. You're funny and clever and very pretty. And you've got legs to die for."

"I just wish I could co-ordinate them better. Let's face it, I'm hardly what you'd call sporty. Honestly, Rosie, Sam can't have liked *anything* about me. He dumped me, remember – sent a text before I'd even got home. How humiliating is that?"

Rosie sighed. "Everyone has dating disasters from time to time. You and Sam just weren't meant to be. You'll laugh about this one day."

Which just goes to show that however nice grown-up people are, they have absolutely no understanding of what it's like to be young.

I could tell Rosie was searching around for more words of wisdom, but before she could relay them her mobile rang. She glanced at the screen and gave me an apologetic look. "Sorry, I'll have to take this, it's work."

Rosie was one of the nicest people I knew and she was the kind of person you could talk to about anything.

She was a nurse and worked in the local hospital, where she'd met Mum when they'd first been students. When Mum and Dad had split up two years ago, she had been there for all of us. She was always a welcome sight on our doorstep with her navy uniform, curly blonde hair, smiling face and kind blue eyes. She was the first person to notice that Will's jeans were wearing out, or that my school skirts were getting too short, and after a quiet word with Dad, it would all be sorted. Last year, Mum moved to London with her new boyfriend. Will and I hadn't wanted to change schools and leave our friends, so we stayed with Dad in term time, and went to Mum's every other weekend and in the holidays. At first I had found it weird, but it's amazing what you get used to.

My best friends, Natalie and Parisa, had been there for me too. Like we always were for each other. Take last night – as soon as I texted them the news that my date had been a major, ten-out-of-ten disaster they had both rushed over. I gazed out of the car window as I replayed our conversation in my head.

"The important question is: did you enjoy yourself?" Parisa asked, breaking off a piece of chocolate from the jumbo-sized bar she had brought for the occasion.

If I was going to be totally honest, the answer to Parisa's question was "No". The date had been awkward and full of embarrassing silences and not a bit like I had imagined it would be in my diary. We had gone for a coffee after school. As soon as we sat down, Sam had started talking about his favourite team, Manchester United, and asking me who I supported. My pretend knowledge of football had evaporated quicker than the froth on my cappuccino.

"I knew I shouldn't have ordered a large coffee." I gestured to Parisa to hand over the chocolate. "It practically came in a bucket. I thought it would look cool and sophisticated, but the massive caffeine hit made me all jittery. I must have seemed like a—"

Will's face appeared round the door. "Hello, girls... talking about us bad boys again?" He put on a girly voice. "I'm telling you! As soon as I saw his face over the cheesy cod bake it was love at first sight..."

I chucked a cushion at the door and we heard him walking off down the landing, laughing to himself.

I turned to Natalie and Parisa. They were both blushing bright red.

Natalie saw my face.

"Oh, come on!" she giggled. "He's funny."

"He's not your brother," I sighed. "Try living with *that* twenty-four hours a day."

"OK, OK. So what did you talk about, *besides* football?"

"I can't remember!" I wailed. "I *do* remember I shredded a lot of paper napkins in a manic nervous way and I kept laughing this stupid fake laugh…"

I demonstrated and they both winced. I put my head in my hands. "Oh God, it was awful… No wonder he dumped me."

"How did you say goodbye?" asked Parisa. "Did he kiss you?"

I blushed at the memory. I think it was more that I had kissed *him*, but I wasn't going to admit that.

"Yes. Sort of."

"Well," prompted Natalie, "what was it like?"

I sighed. "It was … I don't know … not how I imagined," I mumbled, helping myself to another piece of chocolate. I'd been so looking forward to having my first kiss and it had been a major disappointment.

"Was it his kissing technique?" asked Parisa. "Was it rubbish or something?"

I frowned. "I don't think so. But I've nothing to compare it to. It just wasn't a bit like what you say kissing Zack is like." Parisa smiled and tried not to look smug – she and Zack had been an item for ages and we all bowed to her superior knowledge on all snogging-related matters.

"It's just not what I was expecting," I went on.

"Not what you were expecting *how*?" Natalie leaned forward, all ears. She was doing a lot of preparation for her first kiss and was leaving nothing to chance.

"Well, you know how gorgeous he is? I thought I'd look into his blue eyes and it would be all dreamy and thrilling … and more *natural*, somehow. I kind of leaned in and thought, *Here we go…* and he started to kiss me back, but it just felt a bit … well … flat."

"Flat?" Natalie was frowning.

"Well, let's just say I didn't want it to go on for ever."

"So, what are you saying?" said Natalie. "Technically competent kisser, but lacking in dreaminess or thrills?"

"Natalie," I wailed. "You're missing the point. The point is that I kissed Sam Harrison, school heart-throb, and he doesn't want to do it again. In fact, he doesn't want to see me again. And the whole school knows."

"But Sam does this all the time, Emma," said Natalie matter-of-factly. "You know he does. He's been out with loads of girls, but never for very long."

"But I thought I was different! How could I have been so stupid? How could I think I was *special*? And why did I tell *everyone* in school about him asking me out? It's sooo embarrassing."

"Seriously," Parisa soothed, "you're well out of it."

"But I'd like to have been in it for a bit longer than *one* date."

"But only for the sake of your *pride*, Emma." Natalie scrunched up the chocolate wrapper and scored a direct hit into the wastepaper basket. "I'm not exactly getting the 'wow' vibe here. It seems to me you only want to see him again to save face, not because you actually want to spend more time with him."

Parisa nodded. "Natalie's right, Emma. Sam may be gorgeous to look at, but that's not everything. You need to actually like the guy, too, and enjoy his company. It sounds to me as if you just weren't compatible."

I looked at her doubtfully. "I still wish I hadn't told so many people about the date."

"You didn't tell *everyone*," Parisa said loyally.

"That's true. Wasn't the bad-tempered dinner lady off sick yesterday? *She* still might not know," Natalie added, less loyally.

I flashed her a sarcastic smile. "Thanks for that. I *am* aware that everyone knows I am a loser, a rubbish kisser *and* deeply boring."

"Oh, Emma, don't be so hard on yourself. People will have forgotten all about this by the time we get back after Christmas, you'll see."

I managed a weak smile. "Thanks." I sat up a bit taller. "Anyway, I don't know why I thought Sam was so special," I said, trying to sound convincing. "There are plenty of boys just as good-looking. Loads. And I'll be in Austria in a few days' time – I bet it's full of them."

"Definitely!" Natalie cheered. "But remember, it's not just about lust at first sight!"

"OK! I've got the message," I said, though I could see Parisa didn't believe me. "I know what I'm going to do. I'm going to meet a gorgeous Austrian boy and show Sam *and* anyone else who's interested how little I cared about our stupid date…"

And even though I hadn't been *entirely* convinced, just saying it made me feel better.

"Hey, dreamer, the rain's stopping and I've got a warm flat and a hungry cat to get home to." Rosie put her mobile in her pocket and handed me my school bag.

I got out of the car, pulled up my hood, and pressed my face against the driver's window. "Thanks for picking us up, Rosie. I really couldn't face the bus today."

"Don't mention it – my shift was over and I was passing your school anyway. Don't be too down about this Sam thing, will you? It's nearly Christmas. Who knows what Santa may bring?"

I looked up at the low, grey sky. "Some snow would be nice."

"Well, you'll get your wish on that one!" She grinned. "Now go and have a lovely time in Austria – I'm positive this Sam will be nothing but a dim and distant memory when you get back."

"I hope you're right," I said, thinking about my plan to meet my Austrian dream boy on the slopes.

I gave her a quick wave and ran for the door.

"Sharing? With a strange family? Won't that be weird?"

Will had been doubtful when Dad first broke the news.

We had never been away at Christmas before, but this year Mum had to work over the holiday period and so we were staying with Dad for the whole two and a half weeks. Maybe Dad was worried that he couldn't give us as fun a Christmas as we'd had down in London last year, but a week ago he had suddenly gone mad and booked a last-minute skiing holiday in Austria. It sounded brilliant. The only downside was we were sharing the chalet with another family.

Will frowned. "I mean how's that going to work? We're not going to have to share rooms with them or anything, are we? With *strangers*..."

"It'll be fine! Where's your sense of adventure?" Dad replied. "It was a fantastic last-minute bargain, and it'll be fun to meet some new people."

"What do you know about them?" Will asked.

Dad thought for a moment. "Well, there are two parents and I think there are about three children."

"About?!" I shrieked. "Dad, it's so typical of you to be vague about the *most* important thing. How old are they?"

He scratched his head and muttered that he had the details somewhere but, Dad being Dad, he couldn't find them in the piles of papers teetering on his desk. Dad's a journalist and works from home. We had no idea how his great articles and stories emerged from the chaos of his office and found themselves on the front pages of newspapers and magazines, but somehow they did. And sometimes they even won awards.

One thing he wouldn't be winning an award for was organizing a holiday, though. It was a miracle we had got as far as getting off the plane and on to the coach with all our passports, tickets and luggage intact.

I sank back into my seat and stared excitedly out of the window at the distant snowy peaks. I had checked out the other passengers to see if I could spot a family with three children. Three children! I crossed my fingers they would be nice. I was so looking forward to this holiday. True, I'd never skied before, but how hard could it be? And even if I did have a reputation for being the most un-coordinated girl in school, surely falling over on lovely soft snow would be like falling on a feather mattress? I would return with a ton of photos of me with a gorgeous Austrian boy, and then everyone at school would see how little I cared about Sam Harrison. I was just imagining myself in the arms of a tall, handsome skiing champion, when Dad suddenly coughed nervously and leaned across the aisle towards me. "I just want you to know, Emma," he cleared his throat, "that I think this Sam, whatever his name is, sounds a very foolish young man."

I blushed deep scarlet. I could sense Will next to me, trying not to laugh.

"Dad," I pleaded. "I don't want to talk about it. It wasn't anything."

"We-ell, Rosie told me that you were a *little* bit down about the whole thing."

I made a mental note to have a word with Rosie about *that* when I got back.

"No, Dad. I'm fine, really. *Please* can we not talk about it?"

He frowned. "Well, as long as you know that you are a wonderful girl and that just because it doesn't work out with one boy, well … sometimes people just aren't right for each other. But I'm sure there must be hundreds of boys longing to go out with you…"

The girl in the seat in front peered around curiously to check that statement out for herself. She didn't look convinced.

"Thank you for the vote of confidence, Dad," I whispered, "but I would really appreciate it if you would *stop talking about it now.*"

Dad stared at me, and then looked relieved. "Well, OK then, but if you want a chat anytime…"

"Thanks, Dad, but I'm fine."

The conversation had obviously taken a lot out of him because he leaned back in his seat and shortly after began to doze.

Will nudged me.

"Don't you start," I said, but I couldn't help smiling. Dad was always trying to have man-to-man talks with Will, so I knew he understood.

"You never stood a chance with Sam," Will said solemnly. "You weren't wearing footie kit for a start. And I expect you forgot to blow the whistle at half-time and hand out some oranges." He shook his head. "See? Never going to work."

I have to admit when Will's not being a pain he's OK. He's so relaxed about things, whereas I've always got such great expectations about everything. As a result I am mostly doomed to disappointment, whereas he seems to sail straight through life with a big grin on his face. All the girls in our year fancy him, even my two best friends think he's good looking. He's much taller than me, with the same dark brown hair. We've both got the same oval faces, brown eyes and long lashes, but I've got some tiny freckles on my nose.

But the main – and most painful – difference is that lots of girls want to go out with Will and he's never been dumped, whereas I've only had one date in my life and got dumped straight away.

Will nudged me again. "What do you reckon about our chalet mates? Think they'll be any fun?"

I sat up. "Dad said something about the details being in here," I said, rummaging in the bag at my feet.

I pulled out a file and sifted through the pages. "Here it is! Ready to hear who we will be spending our Christmas holidays with?"

"Go on," Will urged.

"Mr and Mrs Temple, and … Mr A Temple, aged fifteen, Miss G Temple, aged thirteen, Miss N Temple, aged seven."

"Great. Not all ankle-biters," Will said enthusiastically.

"Hope Miss G is friendly," I said. "And I hope she hasn't skied before – I don't want to be in the beginners' class on my own. But at least you have skied before, so I won't have to put up with you in my group, flirting with all the girls." I grinned. "So you see, it's not all bad."

"Oh ha ha. Your Christmas present just got *so* much smaller." Will grabbed the file from me. "Now let me guess. Miss G Temple will be an ace skier, a super-model and very smart, and Mr A Temple will be short, fat, slightly sweaty and a little bit desperate. Or of course, it might be the other way round…"

My heart sank. "Yuck! Do you think?"

"No! I bet they'll both be fun."

"I hope so." I sighed.

I wanted to like Miss G. I needed to meet a very special boy on this holiday and it would be easier and a lot more fun with a friend who wanted to meet boys as well. I really hoped that she *wasn't* going to be an ace skier and a super-model.

I hoped she'd be a lot like me.

I glanced beside me at Will, who was now engrossed in the rest of the holiday details. More than anything, I hoped she wouldn't fall for *him*. That would be a disaster. Fingers crossed Will would get on really well with Mr A and leave us girls free to track down some fit Austrian talent...

I pulled my diary and a pen out of my bag and began to fantasize about my first ski lesson. As I wrote, I imagined my tall, tanned, blue-eyed ski instructor, watching me skiing effortlessly down the slope, amazed by my grace and talent. "I cannot believe you have never skied before!" he would cry. "You are a total natural!" And I would glide swiftly down the hardest run like a Bond Girl, with lots of gorgeous boys looking on, wondering who the new mysterious female on the slopes was... I put down my pen and smiled to myself. Everything was going to be fine.

It was very, very cold.

We were standing in front of our chalet. Big fat snowflakes were coming down thick and fast, but in the fading light we could still see that our chalet was beautiful, like an old-fashioned cuckoo clock. After what seemed like hours of winding roads, we had driven up through the little village at the foot of the resort. With just over a week to go till Christmas Day, the village was adorned with twinkling white lights strung across its streets. The shop windows were crammed with decorations, and all the balconies on the buildings were garlanded with evergreen branches and ribbons of red, green and gold. Like the houses and hotels we had just seen in the village, the windows of our chalet had pretty painted shutters and a long wooden balcony upstairs. The roof jutted out over it, and like every roof we had seen, it was thickly covered with snow.

"Dad! It's lovely!" I gasped, trying to catch a flake on my tongue.

"Not bad," Will added. Dad looked pleased with himself.

A tall, white-haired man appeared at the front door. "Welcome! Welcome!" he cried, as snowflakes settled on his beard. "I'm Frank Temple, pleased to meet you. Come on in and meet the family before I turn into a snowman."

Father Christmas, more like, I thought.

As we followed him up the icy path my legs slid from underneath me and I felt myself falling to the ground. Dad grabbed me just in time. I gave him a grateful smile. We dumped our cases in the hall and took off our jackets. Mine was brand new. It was my Christmas present from Mum. I had spent ages choosing it. It was pink with two cool grey zips up the front and thick, dark grey fur around the hood. It matched my grey ski trousers with pink buttons and trim on the pockets perfectly. In the middle of the hall, a staircase entwined with pine branches, gilded pine cones and ivy rose up in front of us. A pale woman with short blonde hair appeared at the top of it. She looked about twenty-five. She had a pretty face, but there was something about her over-bright smile that felt a little false.

"Hello," she said. "You must be the Delamares."

Could this be Mrs Temple? I thought, feeling slightly panicked. Then I remembered the ages of the children and a wave of relief washed over me. She was much too young.

"This is the wonderful Josie." Mr Temple smiled.

Josie came down the stairs and held out her hand. "Hello, I'm your chalet girl for the holiday." She smiled at Dad. "Nice to meet you. I hope you have a very happy holiday. I'll do everything I can to look after you."

Dad beamed. "Thank you very much, Josie, that's very kind of you. Call me Bob." He turned to us. "And this is Will and Emma. We're all really looking forward to our holiday, aren't we?"

Will and I nodded. Josie gave us a fleeting glance before asking Dad to let her know if there was anything he particularly liked to eat, and disappearing into the kitchen.

Mr Temple beckoned us over, and pushed open a door into a spacious sitting room. In one corner stood a large Christmas tree decorated with a few tasteful gold baubles. The walls were wood-panelled, and long, dark red curtains hung at the windows. Thick checked blankets were thrown over the large sofas on each side of the huge fireplace. Facing the crackling fire we could see the backs of two large leather armchairs. The pale blonde head of a young girl, who I guessed to be "Miss N aged seven" slowly appeared over the top of one of them.

"Have you skied before?" she said solemnly, fixing me with a pair of piercing grey eyes.

I looked at Will. "Er, Will has, but I haven't," I replied.

She thought about this, nodded and slowly disappeared again. A large woman got up from the other armchair and laughed. "Please excuse Nina! She hasn't skied before and she's worried about being the only beginner tomorrow. I'm Caroline Temple, pleased to meet you."

"Mum! Nina *knows* I'll be a beginner, too. I haven't skied before either, remember?"

The voice came from a small table in the corner, where a girl with fair hair was flicking through a magazine and a boy was strumming a guitar. Miss G and Mr A, I presumed.

Nina appeared over the top of the chair again, blinked and, without taking her eyes off me, commented, "You don't count, Georgia. I mean proper people."

"I am 'proper people'!" Georgia protested.

"OK, stop it, you two," interrupted Mrs Temple. "You won't be in the same class anyway; Nina will be with the younger ones." Nina opened her mouth to protest. "Where it won't matter if you don't know anyone," her mother carried on, "as you'll soon make loads of friends." She smiled at us and patted her hair absentmindedly. "Sorry about that. It's lovely to meet you." Mrs Temple was warm and motherly with a welcoming smile. "This is Georgia and this Adam," she said, gesturing towards the corner table.

"Hi." Georgia smiled, shyer now that she wasn't talking to her sister.

"Hi." Adam put down his guitar.

"And this is Emma and Will." Dad stepped forward. "They're twins."

I groaned inwardly. Why did everyone always have to mention that?

"Very pleased to meet you." Mrs Temple beamed. "You must be starving after your journey; I know *we* are. We must all sit down, eat, and get to know each other…" She eyed a large box behind one of the sofas. "And there's a little box of Christmas tree decorations to put up as well. We drove here and brought them with us in the car. Josie's decorated the chalet very beautifully, but I thought it would be nice to have some of our own decorations to put up around the place. I know they won't be as tasteful as the ones here," she beamed at Josie, who had just appeared in the doorway, "…but it'll make it feel like home. What do you think?"

We all agreed that it would. Josie managed a tight smile before telling us supper was ready and inviting everyone to sit down. We settled ourselves on the benches on either side of the table. It was laden with baskets of hot bread, a huge pot of chicken casserole and plates of baked potatoes. The adults were all chatting together towards one end, leaving us younger ones at the other. I'd just sat down next to Georgia when Nina determinedly squeezed her skinny frame in between us.

"Scuse me," she said, wriggling herself into position.

She beamed up at me. "I'm so glad you're here. I've only had Georgia to do girl-talk with and she is boring me *to death*..." She looked up the table. "And I've tried to talk to Josie, but she doesn't like children."

"Shhh ... Nina!" Georgia gasped. But Josie hadn't heard. She was hovering by the table, protesting feebly as Dad and the Temples tried to cajole her into joining them.

After one final protest she took a seat. I noticed that although there was a bigger space next to Mrs Temple, she squeezed in on the end next to Dad. Everyone started eating, and at last I had my first chance to get a good long look at Georgia and Adam Temple.

Will and Adam were already chatting away opposite me. I could tell Will thought he had a great girl-chasing partner in Adam. Adam was tall, with shaggy, tawny-gold hair and grey eyes. He looked easy-going and good company – but I hadn't come here to hang out with English boys. I was on a mission. Austrians were *so* much cooler. I was pleased Adam looked fun, though; this meant the boys would hang out together and Georgia and I would be free to meet people without Will's teasing or interference.

However, on the worrying side, I soon realized that although Georgia was incredibly striking, she wasn't the flirty, confident dynamo I had been hoping for. She was pale and slender, with long hair and the same grey eyes as her brother and sister. She was wearing jeans and a sweatshirt and not a hint of make-up.

"Do you go out much at home?" I asked tentatively.

She shook her head. "Not really – only to the library and sometimes out with friends to see a film. I spend most of my time outdoors at weekends, working on … er … projects."

"What kind of projects?"

"Georgia's a scientist," said Nina. "She's crazy about rocks. Her room's full of them."

"Wow." I smiled. "That sounds … um … cool. I think it's great to have a … er … hobby."

Georgia laughed. "It's OK. You don't have to pretend you think it's interesting. I love it, but I don't expect everyone else to. I think I must have got the bug from our granddad – he's a geologist and he works a lot for foreign governments finding new water sources under rocks and mountains."

"Sounds like you're going to be helping to save

the planet one day," I said admiringly.

Georgia blushed. "I hope … well, it is sort of important to me."

"Important!" Nina cried. "You never have any time for anything else."

Nina sighed and leaned towards me. "She'll never, ever find a boyfriend," she whispered. "The boys that are in her rock gang—"

"Geology group!" Georgia interrupted.

Nina ignored her. "The boys that are in her rock gang are all seriously nerdy." She fixed me with her piercing eyes again. "Do you have a boyfriend?"

"Nina! It's rude to ask personal questions." Georgia gave me a sheepish grin over her sister's head. My heart sank. Not because Georgia was obviously brainy and already had an idea about what she actually wanted to do with her life – that was fine – but because now I wasn't sure if she would want to hang out with *me*. Flirting and chasing boys didn't appear to be her scene at all … in fact, at this rate I'd have better luck hanging out with Nina.

I decided to try a different tack. "Do you have boys at your school?"

She shook her head. "No. It's all girls."

"How do you meet boys then?" I asked.

She blushed. "Well, I don't meet many really." She looked at her brother who was still busy talking to Will and lowered her voice. "Though I'd like to."

"Great!" I cried. She looked alarmed by my enthusiasm, so I quickly whispered, "Me too. We're bound to meet *loads* of boys while we're here. I bet there will be some brilliant ones in our ski class."

Nina sniffed. "Hope they like rocks then."

"Stop listening to other people's conversations, Nina," said Georgia, frowning.

"I can't help it!" Nina protested. "I'm sitting right here in the middle. I'm not *invisible*. And I am allowed to *talk*, you know."

Nina turned her back on Georgia and said to me, "Emma, I bet you've had loads of boyfriends. Do you think you could help Georgia get one? She's never had one before."

"What? Me? No!" I gabbled, desperate to get off the subject of boyfriends.

"Oh," Nina said, sounding disappointed.

She crossed her legs under the table, smoothed her

skirt down and leaned into my arm confidentially. "I bet you've kissed tons of boys, haven't you? I've kissed two in my class so far, but not Steven McKay, because he's quite a fast runner. Deep Patel is my boyfriend now. How many boys have you kissed?"

I blushed, because Adam and Will had stopped talking and were listening in.

"No point in asking Emma about that kind of thing, Nina." Will smiled at her kindly. "She's not had a lot of success in that department lately…"

I blushed furiously and glared at him across the table. He wasn't going to say anything about my date with Sam, was he?

"There will be lots of boys in your ski class," Nina said, sticking to her topic. "You could kiss one of them."

Will sighed. "Not very likely."

"Why not?" Nina asked.

"Because the boys in the beginners' class will be too busy falling over and crying like babies and that's not very attractive to big girls."

Nina frowned at me. "Is that true?"

"No, it is *not* true," I replied. "It's just Will being very silly."

Will grinned. "Come on, girls, you might as well face facts – as the ones who have skied before, Adam and I will be in the cool class with the fun people and have the fit girls fighting over us. Which means that we won't have time to help you out by dragging poor, unsuspecting boys back to the chalet or anything. You girls will have to manage all on your own on Planet No Friends."

"Where is Planet No Friends?" Nina asked anxiously. "Are Georgia and Emma going there tomorrow?"

"Yes, Nina, they are," Adam nodded seriously.

"Stop it, Adam," said Georgia. "And just you wait, I bet our class will be stuffed with really gorgeous, amazing people and you'll both be *begging* us to introduce them to you."

"Georgia, Georgia," Adam sighed. "You know as well as I do that your sad, dunces' class will be full of…" he made an "L" shape with his fingers on his forehead, "…loo-sers."

"Ha very ha," I replied sarcastically. Adam was nearly as bad as Will. Nina might have assumed that I'd had a lot more experience with boys than I actually had, but one thing I *did* have experience of was brothers.

"Don't be mean, Adam," Nina responded fiercely. "I bet there *are* nice boys in Emma and Georgia's group. And I bet Emma gets a boyfriend before *you* get a girlfriend."

"You've got to be kidding! No contest," Will cried. "Emma's only had one—"

My heart jumped with alarm.

"Everything all right down there?" Mr Temple interrupted, calling down the table.

"Yes," we all chorused.

Adam leaned forward and his dark grey eyes flashed wickedly at me. "So what do you think?" he asked. "Are you up for the challenge or not?"

"Absolutely!" I found myself replying wildly. "Can't wait!"

Adam grinned. "OK then. Starting at ski school tomorrow ... the race for a date is on."

"Aren't you nervous?" Georgia asked, as we tried on our ski boots in the ski hire shop the following morning. Outside, last night's snow had made everything clean and bright in the morning sunshine and the mountains were dazzling white against the clear blue sky.

"Not at all," I replied, bending my knees and making some swishing movements with my poles. "How hard can it be?"

She giggled as I did some ski-wear model poses in the shop mirror.

Georgia and I had spent a long time getting our winter sports look just right. I had been relieved and delighted when, last night, Mrs Temple had tentatively suggested that instead of Georgia and me sharing with our brothers, Adam could go in with Will, and we could share with each other. We had all jumped at the idea. Nina had sulked because she had wanted to come in with us too, but Mrs Temple told her that she would miss her too much if she didn't sleep in the little bed in her and Mr Temple's room, and she had calmed down.

As soon as we'd woken up, we'd leaped out from under our duvets and hurried over to open the painted shutters, gazing out on the village below us and mountains all around. Then we'd rushed to get ready. Georgia had a dark blue ski jacket and trousers. She'd wrapped a pale blue scarf round her neck and pulled a matching hat down over her fair hair, making her grey eyes look even greyer. Underneath she'd put on a long-sleeved white ribbed sweater and underneath that she was wearing a pale blue thermal top and leggings with a lacy trim.

"These thermals are actually quite pretty," she'd sighed, pulling out a shoulder strap with her thumb. "But *so* hot. I'm boiling already and I haven't moved yet. I think I might take them off."

Her mum had appeared at the door. "Don't you dare! You'll be glad of them when you're on top of the mountain. Now hurry up! Honestly, how long can two girls take to get dressed?!"

Quite a long time, if you have to get your hair tied back just right, put on your mascara and lipgloss and give Georgia some advice on how to wear it – which was, "Wear enough to make a slight difference, but not enough for your dad to notice."

I was really pleased with my new grey ski trousers and close-fitting, pale grey top. Like Georgia, I even liked my new white thermal vest and leggings. We hadn't even made a fuss when we'd had to wear helmets instead of our own hats. We knew we still looked cool.

On the other side of the sunlit valley I could see the early-bird skiers coming down the mountain. Soon I would be joining them, I thought, feeling a rush of excitement. Soon I would be swooshing along with a gorgeous Austrian boy at my side...

"Now, girls," Mrs Temple said, adjusting Nina's boots, "I'm going to collect Nina from her ski school at lunchtime, OK? The dads will meet you at the restaurant at the top of the cable car at half past twelve, but here's some money in case they're late. I'm sure you'll be hungry by then. Josie tells me that your instructor is very experienced, by the way."

Georgia nudged me. "*Very* experienced," she whispered. I got the giggles. Dad, Mr Temple and the boys had already set off, eager to get on the slopes.

"Bye bye, losers," Adam and Will had mouthed as they stomped out of the hire shop in their heavy boots. Georgia and I had stuck out our tongues in retaliation.

Dad and Mr Temple had decided against ski school. They said they'd both skied when they were younger and didn't need lessons. Mrs Temple's normally smiling mouth had gone into a tight line at this, but she'd kept her thoughts to herself.

"Do you think he'll be unbelievably handsome?" I asked, as we stood in the crowded cable car, slowly rising up the mountain. Above us towered the white peaks and a deep blue sky; below us the rocks, trees and snowy ground seemed a very, very, long way down.

"Our ski instructor?" Georgia replied. "Bound to be. They always are, aren't they?"

Once at the top, Mrs Temple deposited us with a gaggle of other nervous-looking youths, all carrying their skis over their shoulders like us.

"Have a good time," she called, as she took Nina off to find her class.

"Yes!" Nina shouted behind her as they went off. "And don't forget to find a boyfriend!"

Georgia and I looked at each other, speechless.

A bark behind us made us both jump. "Hello! You are my beginners' class, yes?'

We turned round. I looked at Georgia. She stared back, open-mouthed. *This* was our ski instructor?

He glided to a halt in front of us. "I am Gunter. I will be your teacher."

"It's ET on skis," Georgia whispered.

"More like Yoda from *Star Wars*," I replied. "And he's definitely not unbelievably handsome."

"More like unbelievably old and wrinkly," Georgia murmured.

"You, in the pink jacket," which was me, "what are you doing? You're looking everywhere but where you should be looking. You keep your eyes on me at all times, understand? That is the way you will learn."

Georgia pulled a face at me.

"Now we put on our skis!" he shouted.

Everyone else seemed to manage this, but it was soon obvious that my skis were not like everyone else's. Each time I tried to lift my boot into place the ski would run away down the slope. In the end Georgia had to hold them steady while I stamped my boots in place.

Gunter eventually got us all into a line and moved

along it checking our boots were clamped on to the skis correctly. I looked around to see what our fellow skiers were like. I was rather depressed to see that the other two girls in our class were seriously pretty. One was standing next to Georgia. She had a heart-shaped face, long blonde hair and perfect skin. I felt a twinge of envy. I had spent ages that morning trying to get my look right and I thought I looked OK, but now I felt it was all in vain. The girl leaned forward and gave Georgia and me the friendliest smile.

"Hi, you are English? I am Lenka, I am from Slovakia. Are you feeling afraid?"

We grinned. "We are," we chorused.

I immediately felt cross with myself for being jealous of her looks. She seemed really nice.

There were only four boys in our group. Three of them were Austrians. My heart sank when I realized that they were all about eleven or twelve years old. I wasn't going to meet my fantasy Austrian boy *here*, that was for sure. The fourth boy was English and looked about our age.

He smiled shyly. "Hi, I'm Gordon." He waved a ski pole. He wasn't what you would call good-looking, but he had a friendly face. "Pretty hard to get the hang of this skiing thing, isn't it?" He frowned as his skis splayed outwards making him look like a giraffe at a watering hole. "Outdoor sport's not really my thing." I nodded in sympathy.

The second girl sneered and leaned forward on her ski poles. "Oh yeah? And what *is* your *thing*?" She spoke with an American accent. She had a tanned face, with long, shiny chestnut hair, huge dark eyes and a large lipsticked mouth. She wore expensive-looking white trousers and her matching jacket was trimmed with thick white fur.

Gordon flushed. "Er … well, I like science, and um … geology and stuff like that."

The girl turned away with a huge yawn.

"Well, *she's* rude," I heard someone whisper.

I turned to see two new girls standing behind us. One was tall and lanky in a silver ski jacket, and the other was shorter, and wearing all black. They saw me and smiled.

"Hi, I'm Dizzy," said the taller one, shuffling forward to introduce herself. She had shoulder-length blonde hair and slightly protruding pale blue eyes.

"And I'm Bella." Her dark-haired friend giggled. "And isn't this ski instructor just so *totally* not what you had imagined? He's like the hideous matron of our house at boarding school, isn't he, Dizzy?"

"*Absolutely*. Oh God, this is going to be hell and torture," she groaned, as Gunter finished checking the last Austrian boy's skis and skied back to face us. "How are we going to bear a week of this?"

"Stop talking!" Gunter barked. "Now, everyone watching me, we will go slowly, practising our snow plough." He placed his skis in an upside down "V" shape. "Everybody straighten up in the line, please."

The American girl in the white jacket glided sideways and drifted slowly down the nursery slope.

"What are you doing?" Gunter shouted after her.

"I don't know! And don't yell at me!" she screeched. "This ski suit cost a fortune. If I fall and tear it I'm going to—" There was a scream as, ski poles flailing, she flopped backwards on to her expensive behind. She remained on the ground and banged her poles in the snow. "Aaaargh! I hate this already!" She glanced back at the rest of us, who were just managing to stay upright. "And what are you people staring at?"

We all turned away and tried to look casual, stifling our giggles. Gunter helped her back to our line and we set off again like a row of awkward ducklings. All except Lenka, who was obviously a natural.

The American girl lost control again and barged into Georgia. "Get out of my way," she snapped.

Georgia opened her eyes wide. "Well, excuse *me*." She swerved out of the way, desperate to avoid another collision and skied straight into my path. I tripped over her skis and fell flat on my face. And that was just the beginning.

It didn't take long for me to realize that I was not going to be a Bond Girl skiing swiftly down the slopes. It seemed the mouthy American and I had something in common. We were both absolutely rubbish at skiing. And let me tell you, snow might look soft, but when you've fallen on to it a couple of hundred times it sort of loses its bounce. I hobbled out of the lesson at the end of the morning in agony.

"You do better tomorrow if you look at me and not all the time searching for the boys," Gunter barked. He had a point. I had kept my eyes peeled for my Austrian dream boy, but so far I hadn't seen him.

I took off my helmet, then grappled with my skis, or, as I now saw them, instruments of torture, and put them on the rack outside the restaurant with everyone else's.

"I will never be able to get the hang of it," I sighed.

"Honestly, you will." Dizzy smiled. "We've been here for a week now and it does get easier."

Bella saw my puzzled look. "We arrived last week and said we'd skied before," she explained, "which was true – we went with our school last year. So they put us in a higher class. But what we didn't say was that we were totally useless at it. We've been demoted twice, so now Gunter has us at his mercy! But at least we've met you guys. Are you going to the restaurant for lunch? Pretty much everyone meets up there and—" She stopped because the American girl had just appeared.

"I'm going to get my mom to get that guy fired," she raged, knocking the snow off her boots. We eyed her warily. She'd done nothing but whine and complain all morning. And nothing was ever her fault. When she had fallen over at the bottom of the slope, miles from anyone else, she had complained it was the glare from Dizzy's silver jacket that had blinded her.

"I can't believe he's allowed to treat us like that."

She delved into her pocket, took out a lipgloss and applied a thick coat. "I'm Janine, by the way. Are you guys going to the restaurant?"

Georgia and I looked at Bella and Dizzy, but nobody moved.

"Come on, let's go. I'm not meeting my mom for half an hour."

I glanced around and noticed Lenka nearby, talking to a man who was obviously her dad.

"Do you want to come with us?" I called over. She may have been unbearably pretty, but she was also very nice; she had helped me to my feet loads of times this morning.

She nodded enthusiastically.

Janine looked irritated. "Let's go, then!" she snapped impatiently. We all crunched after her, trying to get used to walking in our heavy ski boots.

There was no sign of the dads when we went in, so Georgia and I ordered frankfurters and chips and went outside on the terrace. We found a big empty table in a sheltered corner, draped with a blue checked tablecloth. I sat down and pushed my shades up on top of my head. The view across the mountain was breathtaking. I felt on top of the world in spite of my disastrous morning and aching limbs. Dizzy, Bella, Lenka and Janine clumped over to join us. Nearby, Gordon sat with his parents, but it was obvious that he'd much rather have been with us. I was glad it was all girls at our table, though, because we could talk about anything we wanted. And I was glad that the dads hadn't turned up yet, either. We girls had serious things to discuss.

"So," Janine squirted ketchup on to her chips, bringing me back to earth, "you've been here a week already?" she said, talking to Dizzy and Bella. "What's the boy situation? Seen anybody interesting?"

Dizzy sighed. "Well, there is one completely gorgeous Austrian boy that we are both totally in love with, aren't we, Bella?"

Bella nodded vigorously. "Totally. But he's been going *up* the ski classes as we've been coming down them and we keep missing him. He doesn't eat here at lunchtime either, but we've seen him in the village with his family."

"What's so special about him?" Georgia asked.

Bella and Dizzy looked at each other.

"Cute, shoulder-length blond hair," Dizzy began.

"Green, green eyes," Bella continued.

"Tall."

"Fit."

"Tanned."

"Shy smile to die for."

"We love him!" they chorused.

Lenka and I joined in as they collapsed into giggles.

"He sounds worth checking out," Janine said coolly. "Anyone else?"

"Hmmm … there were lots of cute boys last week, but they've all gone home. We're on the lookout for new talent."

Janine suddenly nudged me hard. "And here it is," she hissed.

I looked across the terrace – it was crowded with people so I couldn't see who she was talking about. All I could see were Adam and Will, who were wandering around with their trays, looking for somewhere to sit.

Janine leaned forward and whispered, "I think they've noticed us."

"Who?" Georgia and I asked at the same time.

"Those boys! Right there! Are you two blind?"

I followed her gaze. She was pointing at Adam and Will.

Georgia and I exchanged horrified looks. "You must be joking!"

"What's wrong with them? They're definitely the best-looking boys I've seen since I got here."

The other girls all nodded in agreement.

"They've got *terrible* personalities," I said firmly.

"That is so *very* true," Georgia added.

"Trust me, you wouldn't want to know them," I continued. "They are sooo boring … I mean, really, incredibly dull."

"You've met them already?" Janine gasped.

"Actually, they're our brothers," Georgia admitted.

"And I hate to disappoint you, but they won't sit with us. We absolutely, positively know that for a fact."

But I was wrong. Will was making a beeline for our table and Adam, beaming broadly, was following close behind.

"Hello!" Will grinned. "Had a good morning?" I looked around. Was he talking in this pleasant fashion to *me*? "I'm Will," he went on, addressing the others, "Emma's brother, and this is Georgia's brother, Adam."

"Hi!" said Adam. "Room for a couple more?" I couldn't help noticing that he had caught the sun, making his eyes seem an even more intense grey. He scanned the table.

Janine gave both of them a dazzling smile. "Sure there's room for you. Come and join us."

Adam put down his tray and pulled up a chair next to Lenka. Will sat down next to me. I coughed quietly.

"What are you doing, Will?"

"Sitting down, sis, as you do to have lunch." He looked around and frowned, "This *is* a restaurant, isn't it? You know, a place where you buy stuff and eat…"

"I *know* what a restaurant is, Will." I snapped. "I just didn't think you'd want to be hanging out here with us. You know, the *beginners*?" I said pointedly.

"Don't you mean the *losers*, Emma?" Georgia added, even more pointedly, staring meaningfully at Adam.

The other girls looked confused.

Adam laughed nervously. "We were only kidding, I don't care what ski class people are in – the important thing is to be friendly, isn't it?" He gave Lenka his most charming smile and poured out a drink. "You must meet some of the people in *our* ski class."

I looked around. "And where are they?"

"Still skiing. Actually…" Adam tried to look casual, "…we're all boys in our class."

"Oh, *really*?" Georgia and I chorused. Suddenly everything was so much clearer.

"So you thought you'd come and have lunch with us? That is *so* Adam." Georgia smiled at the other girls. "We're *so* close."

But Adam wasn't listening; he was staring over the terrace at a commotion taking place below us. I stood up to see what he was looking at. There were two skiers coming down the mountain with a stretcher on a sledge. They were nearly at the restaurant.

Adam leaned out as far as he could over the balcony, then he suddenly let out a great shout.

"Hey, hey! Stop! What's happening! Stop!"

"What are you *doing*?" Will cried, embarrassed. "Enough with the yelling!"

Adam turned to Will, a look of shock on his face. "On the stretcher, didn't you see?"

"No." Will was looking anxious now. "Why, who was it?"

"I'm sure it was your dad," Adam replied.

"Are you *sure?*" I asked, my eyes filling with tears.

Adam nodded.

Will jumped to his feet. "Come on! We've got to catch them up."

Adam put his hand out to stop him. "Hey, wait up, it's not going to help anyone if you go crashing down the mountain and get hurt, too. Those paramedics are expert skiers and will be going down the fastest route, which might not be one we can ski. They'll be taking him to a doctor, so why don't we go down in the cable car and find out where the medical centre is?"

"It'll take too long," Will cried, pushing past Adam and running down the steps to the ski rack.

"Stop, Will!" I yelled, chasing after him, which was very hard in ski boots.

"Whoa! What's happening?" Mr Temple skidded to a halt in front of us in a spray of ice and snow. I felt a wave of relief to see his bear-like presence.

"Adam saw Dad being stretchered off the mountain." Will was frantically strapping on his skis.

"That's right," said Mr Temple. "But he's going to be OK. I was with him when he had the accident. He decided to be rather … er … over ambitious, took a turn on a difficult run too fast, and fell. I had a good look at the damage and he's broken his ankle."

"How d'you know?" Will asked. "Are you a doctor?"

Mr Temple nodded. "Yes, I am. I'm a professor of orthopaedics, otherwise known as a 'Bone Doctor'. And I can tell you that your father has a broken ankle, a very small fracture, I would guess, nothing more. Terribly bad luck, of course. I did tell him to take it easy on the first day, but…"

"Dad never listens," I said, nodding. Another wave of relief flooded over me. "Poor Dad. We'd better go down and try and cheer him up. We can at least keep him company while he's getting his plaster put on. What a rubbish Christmas holiday *he's* going to have."

We got into the cable car with Mr Temple. Georgia and Adam had offered to come with us, but there was no point in all of us going. Georgia gave me a big hug. "See you soon," she said. "I hope he's OK."

Four hours later we were back at the chalet and Dad was lying on one of the sofas under a blanket with his leg in plaster up to his knee.

"Do you want me to get your book, Dad?" I asked. "Or perhaps you'd like something to drink?"

"I've got his book here," Josie said briskly. "And I've just put the kettle on. Why don't you leave things to me, Emma – it's much easier as I know where everything is."

It irritated me that someone I'd only just met was acting as if they knew Dad better than I did. As soon as we'd arrived last night, Josie had been super-attentive towards Dad, and when she'd found out at supper that he was a writer she'd been even more excited and impressed. I had noticed her talking to him intently at breakfast this morning as well.

"What about your notepad, Dad?" Will suggested.

"Josie's found it already." Dad smiled, holding it up. "She's amazing!"

Feeling a bit useless, Will and I sat down with Nina and Mrs Temple and began to sort out the Christmas decorations, which we'd ended up leaving last night.

Georgia and Adam arrived home soon after and joined us in adding the Temples' wacky home-made and mismatched decorations to the tree.

Josie didn't say anything, but it was obvious she wasn't pleased. "Great, now it really feels like Christmas!" she said, clapping her hands and plastering an over-bright smile on her face.

"Do you know, it turns out Josie wants to be a writer," Dad informed us, as he watched Mrs Temple balance a wobbly angel made from an empty loo roll and paper doilies on top of the tree. "She's written a book that she's trying to get published. She just needs a break."

"Looks like she's found one, then," Will said, unravelling some fairy lights.

Dad frowned, then smiled when he realized the joke. "No seriously, you should show it to me sometime, Josie," he said. "I'd be happy to take a look and give you my opinion. And I'll have plenty of time on my hands now. I'm sure you'll be sick of the sight of me soon."

"I don't think so. You'll probably get sick of the sight of *me*," Josie gushed.

"I am already," Will whispered to me. "I wish she was as nice to the rest of us as she is to Dad."

I nodded. Suddenly, the thought of Dad stuck in the chalet every day with Josie began to make me feel rather uneasy. At once I told myself not to be so ridiculous – she couldn't be interested in Dad. I knew people thought he was good-looking – he was tall, with thick hair like Will's and smiley brown eyes – but surely he was way too old for her.

"Come on, Emma." Georgia came over to where I was sitting and nudged me with her foot. "Up on your feet. Here's a load of tinsel – get decorating. And Nina, tinsel is for the tree, not for your head."

"I'm a princess. I'm crowning myself. Because I was the best skier in my group."

"Nina! Don't boast," cried Mrs Temple.

"I'm not boasting, it's true."

Nina reluctantly stood still long enough for her mum to unravel her tinsel crown and remove the two gold baubles she had looped round her ears.

"Well, good for you, Nina," I replied. "I wish I could say the same. But sadly I was bottom of my class and I spent most of the lesson on my bottom … which means, I'm afraid, that I can't help decorate the tree."

"Why not?" Will was now standing on a chair, being fed a long coil of fairy lights by Mr Temple.

"Because I'm too weak and in too much pain. I've totally seized up. In fact, I may never walk again."

"Really? Poor you. Is it that bad?" Adam crouched down in front of me, a serious expression on his face.

"Ye-es," I replied, a little warily.

"Is it just your legs?" His eyes were staring into mine, full of concern.

"Mmmm … kind of all over agony, really. But legs, definitely."

"Here?" he asked, gently placing both hands round my ankle.

"Er…" I began, but before I could finish he began to shake my whole leg up and down.

I shrieked in surprise. Will and Georgia burst out laughing.

"Or this one?" He grabbed the other one and shook it from side to side.

I kicked out. "Get off me, you sadist!" I yelled, trying to scrabble backwards and get free. Which is difficult when you're laughing too.

"Perhaps your arms...?" He lunged forward, but I was up on my feet by now and as he dived after me I flung myself behind the sofa, leaving him face down in the cushions.

"Seems you've made a miraculous recovery," Georgia observed, giggling.

"Your brother is a sick and cruel person," I said, crawling out from behind the sofa on all fours. "He brings shame on your family."

"Well, that's true," she sighed. "Here, have some tinsel."

"I think your brother's going to win our little bet, hands down," I sighed as I flopped on to my bed. The evening had just ended with the official switching on of the Christmas tree lights. My first morning on the slopes seemed a long time ago. Now that I had some time to think about it, I had to admit that it hadn't gone as well as I'd hoped where both skiing *and* boys were concerned. Most of the girls in our ski class had been fun, though, and of course there was Georgia – the more time I spent with her, the more I realized how lucky I was to be sharing a chalet with her. We hadn't stopped talking all morning, and in the brief periods between falling over, we had discussed our mutual desire to find romance while we were on holiday. I had told her about wanting to meet my dream Austrian boy ... though I had been a bit vague about exactly why. I wasn't ready to tell her about the Sam Harrison disaster just yet. I rolled over to face her, wincing in pain at my aching limbs.

"Did you see *anyone* cool this afternoon?" I asked. "I know you said you spent it goofing around with the girls from ski school on the nursery slopes, but did anyone catch your eye? Or is this the one ski resort in Austria with no good-looking boys in it?"

"Will you just stop moaning for a minute and listen," Georgia said, her eyes shining brightly. "I've got some news I've been dying to tell you all evening."

I sat up. "What? You're looking all excited. What's up?"

"Guess who I saw this afternoon?"

"Who?"

"The Austrian boy, that's who. The one that Dizzy and Bella were talking about."

"And is he as gorgeous as they described?"

"Better!" said Georgia, smiling. "Honestly, Emma, he is your dream boy. He skied right past us as Adam and I were waiting to come down in the cable car. And guess what?"

"What?"

"When he went past, Adam said, 'Oh, there's Franz; he's in our ski class.' Just like that!"

I grinned to myself. Franz. That was *exactly* the kind of name my Austrian dream boy would have. "Did you say anything?" I asked.

"No. I just said, 'Oh, really,' completely casually."

"Brilliant. We mustn't let Adam and Will know we want to meet him."

"You want to meet him, not me!" cried Georgia. "You're the one with the Austrian fixation."

"OK, OK, it's me that wants to meet him. But how am I going to do that? Dizzy said he always goes for lunch with his family, and I'm never going to bump into him during the day unless he decides to hang out on the nursery slopes, which, let's face it, isn't very likely."

Georgia frowned. "Well, we're just going to have to think of a very brilliant plan, aren't we?"

6

"No." I shook my head. "I'm not doing it."

Georgia and I were standing at the bottom of the chairlift watching the queue of skiers waiting to get on.

We had finished ski school early due to Janine insisting she had done some serious damage to her leg and wailing her head off. It was obvious she hadn't, but I wasn't going to argue. I was thrilled the agony was over early. The others had gone straight to the restaurant and we'd agreed to meet them there later.

"Look, Emma. Do we want to go up high, where the good-looking boys are?" Georgia asked, "or do we want to stay on our little nursery slope for ever, with eleven-year-olds who still think farting is funny and stare at our chests the whole time?"

"What about Gordon?" I said desperately. "He's nice, and he likes scientific things, like you. He could be your perfect match – let's face it you've got a lot in common," I finished weakly.

Georgia narrowed her eyes at me, so I shut up and turned to observe the next couple of skiers getting into position on the chairlift. A chairlift is on a continuous loop, so you have to be ready and move fast, or it continues relentlessly up the mountain without you, or, even worse, with only half of you attached. I watched as the next empty chair whirred slowly down the mountain towards us, turning round the huge cog at the end. It came back round and rumbled on towards the backs of the waiting couple. Just as it was about to knock them flying, they sat back and the chair scooped them up. *Whoosh!* They pulled down the overhead safety bar and they were off up the mountain, their chair swinging from a thin-looking cable. I gazed up at their dangling skis as they got smaller and smaller.

I shook my head.

"I can't, Georgia. I'm too scared. I fell off the T-bar lift *twice* just getting this far. If it hadn't been for that kind man I'd still be stranded somewhere down there." I pointed vaguely down the valley.

She gave me a look. "It's *your* choice, Emma – meeting a gorgeous Austrian boy or being sad losers … remember *my* dream boy might be up there, too."

That decided it. "We have to do it, don't we?"

Georgia nodded. "We do."

We both looked up at the chairlift again.

"Do you think we'll die?" I asked.

"Probably. But it'll be worth it. And if we do make it, we won't actually have to ski when we get to the top – we'll just stand around in the snow and act casual."

I raised my eyebrows. "For a girl who told me she hardly went out and didn't know many boys, you've certainly picked up speed lately."

Georgia giggled. "It's not like I *didn't* want to meet them. It's meeting someone like you, you know, who's got loads of experience. I feel so much more confident because you know what you're doing."

I gave her an anxious smile. I knew I was going to have to tell Georgia about my disastrous one and only date with Sam soon, but I couldn't help liking the feeling that *someone* believed I had lots of experience with boys. And now wasn't the time for confessions. I took a deep breath. "Come on, then. Let's do it."

We joined the queue and at last it was our turn. My heart was pounding as the man steadying the chairs beckoned us forward. We shuffled into position, and with bums poised in a semi-sitting position, we turned to watch the empty chair coming up behind us. Then with a bump and a loud clang we felt ourselves being lifted up off the ground. Georgia frantically pulled the bar down and, swinging terrifyingly, we rose up the mountain. I gripped my ski poles with one hand and held tightly on to the thin bar with the other – it was the only thing stopping us from falling down on to the jagged mountain below.

I turned to Georgia. "You can open your eyes now. I think if we keep absolutely and totally still and don't look down, we should be all right."

She opened one eye, then the other and breathed deeply. "Phew! Well, that wasn't so bad, was it?"

"Wasn't it?"

She gave me a confident smile. "Now, look at us sitting on the chairlift as cool as you like. I can even bear to look down. Whoa! That is far." She caught her breath and risked another glance. "Hey, just look at those skiers! That could be us by the end of the holiday." She watched for a while and then suddenly clapped her hand over her mouth. "Oh, I don't believe it! That's a total, utter disaster."

"What's a disaster?" I wailed.

"Franz just went past on his way down the mountain. We've come all the way up here for nothing."

"Nooooo!" I yelled. "You're not serious?"

"No, I'm not." She grinned. "Only kidding."

"If I had the courage to lift my hand off this bar, I'd strangle you with it."

We sat in silence for a moment taking in the view.

"Why Austrian?" she asked suddenly.

"What do you mean?"

"Why is it so important that it's an Austrian boy? I mean, you'll see for yourself that he's totally gorgeous and everything, and I know you've got your mind set on him, but you won't *really* know what he's like until you meet him, will you? He might be really boring. Looks aren't everything, are they?"

I knew what she was saying was true – Natalie and Parisa had said something very similar. But in my head, my dream boy was Austrian. I'd been thinking about him so much I already *did* know him in my imagination. He was romantic and cool and we could talk about anything for hours. Everyone at school would be impressed and that hurtful memory of being dumped by Sam Harrison would be wiped out for good. Another boring English boy just wouldn't do.

"I can't really explain," I said, trying to dodge the question. "But I'm not changing my mind. The boy for me *has* to be Austrian."

"Well, I'm glad I'm not so specific. If I get on with a boy of any nationality and he gets on with me, then that's fine."

I grinned at her. "Well, good luck to both of us, then. Look, we're nearly there."

The thing about the chairlift not stopping is that it's OK at the bottom, where you're standing on a platform on a flat surface, but as we watched the skiers in front we realized that it isn't like that at the top. You have to tip yourself off on to a *very* steep little slope and ski off fast. I quickly worked out that if I bottled out of attempting this I would be cranked round the huge wheel at the top and sent off back down the mountain again.

"He's here!" Georgia jabbed her elbow into me. "Franz is right there, standing by the chairlift, talking to Adam."

"If you're kidding me again…"

"No, look!"

I risked a quick glance. My heart skipped a beat as I caught sight of a gorgeous boy with shoulder-length blond hair and a lovely smile. There was no doubt about it – he was absolutely, positively the one.

"Emma, concentrate, we're here," Georgia hissed through gritted teeth as she lifted the bar. "Remember what Gunter said: bend the knees… Ready, steady, GO!"

We stood up and launched ourselves forward.

I'm not really sure what happened next. I must have fallen over my skis or something, as one minute I was careering down a very steep slope, my arms flailing in a desperate attempt to balance, and the next minute my face was planted in the snow. The pain I could live with. But the humiliation and embarrassment were another thing. This was not the introduction I had planned. As I lay with my face in the snow I decided the best thing to do was to stay where I was. Hopefully, they hadn't noticed me and would soon have skied off down the mountain, leaving me to get back on my feet in private.

"Emma?" I recognized Adam's voice. I could just see his ski boots out of the corner of my eye. I didn't move.

"Emma?"

I waved my fingers in a "Hi, I'm kind of busy right now" way, but otherwise remained motionless.

"Are you OK, Emma?" It was Georgia.

"Is your friend OK?" an Austrian voice enquired.

"Emma?" This time Adam's face was right next to mine, so close I could feel his breath on my cheek. "What's the matter?"

I sighed. They obviously weren't going to go away. I rolled over and attempted to sit up, which wasn't very easy with my skis attached to my feet.

"Hello," I said, with as much dignity as I could muster, brushing some snow out of my hair.

I could see Adam was trying not to laugh. I glared at him furiously and he pulled himself together.

"I'm not sure what you two are doing this far up the mountain, but isn't it rather a long way from your beginners' class?" He stood up. "This is Franz, by the way … Franz, this is my sister Georgia, and…" he looked down at me sitting in the snow, "…this is Emma."

I looked up and found myself gazing into the greenest eyes I've ever seen.

"Hello, Franz," I croaked.

Meeting Franz had made me realize two things: firstly, he was definitely the boy who was going to make the Sam Harrison disaster disappear from my mind for ever; and secondly, that I was never, ever going back up the mountain again. Not on that chairlift. After our much too brief introduction, Franz had disappointingly skied off to meet his family in the village. Will had then arrived, skidding to a halt right in front of us and showering everyone with snow. He and Adam were desperate for lunch, so Georgia and I had had no choice but to go straight back down the mountain.

The only problem was that I didn't fancy the small gondola lift that took you back down. I had had enough of swinging above mountains for one day. "And I need the skiing practice more than anyone," I pleaded. Will refused to help me ski down, as he sensitively said he was starving and it would take ages...

"Don't think I don't know it's because you've got

to make up for missing lunch and possible flirting time yesterday," I said. "Thanks for putting your own sister first, by the way. I really appreciate it."

"Don't mention it." Will grinned. "And haven't you got someone you'd like to see, Adam?" Will winked at him.

"Not officially." Adam's cheeks flushed.

"Well, I've got some catching up to do, so if you don't mind…" Will looked at Georgia and me.

"Speaking for myself," Georgia said decisively, "I'd rather risk the gondola than try and get down on skis."

"Great," Will cried. "Sorted! Let's go!" And he grabbed Georgia's arm and pulled her towards the lift.

Which left Adam and me, standing in the snow, looking at each other.

I winced. "Looks like you're saddled with me. Sorry if it's messed up your love life."

"Yeah, right, of course you are," he said, grinning and zipping up his jacket. The sun had gone in and it was starting to snow. "I know you did it on purpose. It's clear to me that you'd do anything to win a bet."

"That's not true – trust me, this is the last place I want to be," I said, as I fumbled to adjust the straps on my helmet. "So, let me guess … I reckon it's Lenka."

"Do you now?" He took off his gloves, stuffed them under his arm and sorted out my straps. "What makes you think that?"

"Totally obvious. She's unbelievably pretty and really nice … and you made a beeline for her at lunch yesterday. She's the perfect girlfriend."

Adam raised an eyebrow. "Really? Well, thanks for your insightful comments. Come on, let's go."

Adam set off down the slope, and I followed slowly behind, my skis in a permanent snowplough. "You'd be so lucky if she agreed to go out with you," I shouted after him.

"Thank you, I'm touched," he yelled back.

"Don't mention it," I said and promptly fell over. He skied over to help me up.

"I swear my skis are the most slippery kind ever made." I staggered to my feet.

"Hmmm. That would be it," he grinned. I tried to hit him with my ski pole, but immediately ended up sitting in the snow again.

"I'm sorry," I said. "This skiing thing … I don't think I'm a natural…"

"*You don't say!*" he laughed, grabbing hold of my hands and pulling me towards him. I stood up, overbalanced and cannoned into him, knocking him over backwards and landing on top of him.

"What *are* you a natural at?" he asked as I clambered off him, my cheeks red with embarrassment; I knew it was only Adam, but it was still a ground-open-up-and-swallow-me moment. I staggered up again, trying to get my skis to face the right way.

"Lots of things," I snapped. "Though not necessarily anything snow and ice-related. And that was your fault. You pulled too hard."

He nodded. "Just follow me – we're going to go really slowly. You can do this. You're going to be fine."

Then I felt bad. "Thanks, Adam, I know you'd rather be down in the restaurant with the others. You should have just left me. I would have got down on my own eventually."

I began to slide and he grabbed my arm.

"Sure," he smiled. "Come on, Bambi, let's get moving."

Inch by inch, we made our way down the mountain, as faster skiers swished past on either side. At last, after what seemed like hours, the restaurant came into sight, but there was no sign of Will or the others. I looked at my watch – it was almost two o'clock. They would have finished their lunch ages ago.

"I reckon Will will have beaten us all to the first date," Adam said, pulling off his helmet.

"That's because he's not as picky as the rest of us," I sniffed. I unclipped my skis and slung them over my shoulder.

Adam shrugged. "Well, now that we're here, do you fancy a hot chocolate? You must be pretty cold after that little escapade."

I shook my head. "I think I've had enough for one day. I'm going to go back to the chalet and have a nice hot bath. But seriously, thanks for getting me down – I really appreciate it. I hope you catch up with the others, and good luck with Lenka." I smiled.

"No problem." He turned and headed for the restaurant. "See you later."

And as I trudged towards the cable car I knew I really meant those words. It had suddenly dawned on me that if Adam and Lenka were an item it would mean she wouldn't be interested in Franz. Because if she was, I knew I wouldn't stand a chance.

As soon as I got back to the chalet I went upstairs and had a long soak in the bath. The journey down the mountain had taken every ounce of my courage and stamina, and my whole body ached like crazy.

Dad was in the sitting room playing Snap with Mrs Temple and Nina, and although they invited me to join in, all I wanted to do was lie on my bed and think about Franz. Georgia was right. He was my perfect dream boy. He was absolutely and totally gorgeous, and I couldn't wait to see him again. The only question was when? With me stuck in the beginners' class for ever, and Franz never being around at lunchtime, we were destined never to cross paths.

I must have drifted off because the next thing I knew, Georgia was shaking me awake. "Oi, sleepyhead, wake up, we've got plans!"

I sat up, rubbing my eyes. "We have?"

"Yep. Will has had the great idea of suggesting a sledging party and we're all meeting up ... including Franz!"

"We are? Quick, tell me everything! What did

you get up to this afternoon?"

"There's not much to tell – honestly, Emma. We were all together at lunch – me, Dizzy, Bella, Janine, Lenka, plus Will and this Austrian girl, Marina, he met in the queue. She was telling him about a great place for sledging just outside the village and he suggested going later on this afternoon. And then he met up with the boys from his ski class after lunch, including Franz, and some of them are coming along too."

I couldn't believe it – for once in his life, Will had had a brilliant idea.

"Thank you, Will," I sighed. "And true to form, it sounds as if he's found himself a date already."

Georgia nodded. "And he might not be the only one. Adam turned up when we girls were messing about on the nursery slopes this afternoon, and he and Lenka were getting on pretty well. I think you're going to have to move fast if you're going to win the dating bet!"

I grinned. Thanks to my brother I now had the perfect opportunity to meet Franz … and with a bit of luck he might even ask me out tonight. I couldn't help thinking that I was well on my way to my dream date. I wondered if Adam was thinking the same thing, too.

"What about *your* dream boy, Georgia?" I asked, as we got ready to go out.

"I've not seen him yet," she replied, applying some lipgloss. She was now quite an expert at using this and my mascara. "But I'm hopeful."

"What about Gordon?"

"No."

"But he's into science and he's really nice."

"No. Again."

I held my hands up in the air, laughing. "OK, just asking. We'll have to see what these other boys from Adam and Will's ski class are like."

Georgia grinned. "I'll know the perfect boy when he comes along, but until then I'm just going to enjoy myself and have some fun with our new friends."

"I know *my* dream boy has come along. He's the most gorgeous boy ever and—"

"Stop judging Franz on his looks!" Georgia laughed, drawing back to look at her reflection. "You haven't actually spoken to him yet, apart from 'Hello'."

"You're right, but trust me, I just know he's the one." I glanced across at her. "I don't think we need any blusher – we've got colour in our cheeks from being outdoors all day."

I looked at myself in the mirror – new skinny jeans, pretty blue T-shirt and mini cardigan – and sighed as I pulled on a huge navy jumper. Sadly, sledging is not an activity for flirty dresses and high heels.

"How do I look?" Georgia asked.

She was wearing her black jeans and I had lent her a dark grey shirt, which really brought out the colour of her eyes. Her long fair hair was tied back with a thin white ribbon, and she had stolen Adam's black ribbed sweater to wear on top. She looked great.

"Wow, Georgia, you look stunning. Let's hope you meet someone as gorgeous as Franz."

"I keep telling you," she protested, "I don't care about gorgeous, I care about getting on with people. Georgia to Emma, are you receiving me?"

"Loud and clear," I replied.

"Good, let's go sledging, then. Excited?"

"Like you can't imagine."

I nearly fainted when Franz appeared.

We were meeting up on a slope outside one of the big hotels.

He loped along the path towards us pulling a sledge behind him. He was wearing dark jeans tucked into big sheepskin-lined boots, his blond hair tucked under a black pull-on hat. "Hello." He gave us a smile that lit up his gorgeous green eyes.

I opened my mouth, but no words came out.

"Hello," Georgia replied, saving the day. "Looking forward to sledging?"

"Definitely!" He grinned. "You are Will and Adam's sisters, yes?"

"We are!" I cried. "But please don't hold that against us."

There was an awkward pause – clearly my joke had not translated well. "Ooh, look, I think everyone's here," said Georgia quickly. "I can't wait to get going!"

We'd found three sledges in the boot room under our chalet. Nearly everyone else had managed to get their hands on one too. All except Janine, which was odd as she was staying with her diamond-encrusted mother in the most luxurious chalet in the ski resort, which she'd boasted had everything.

"I just couldn't find one," she drawled, "so I'm hoping someone will share with me." She batted her heavily made-up eyes at Franz. He smiled warily, and quietly started up a conversation with Hamish and Ian, the other boys from Adam and Will's ski class. Hamish and Ian were both huge and Scottish and seemed like fun, but I could see instantly that Georgia wasn't the least bit interested in either of them. Luckily, Dizzy and Bella were, and they soon joined in the conversation.

Just as I was edging closer to Franz, Marina, Will's Austrian date, turned up. She'd obviously met Franz before and they immediately began to chat away in German.

I sighed – was I ever, *ever*, going to get a chance to talk to him?

After much standing around, Marina and Will went off to sledge and so did Gordon and Georgia.

Dizzy leaped on to Ian's sledge and Hamish went happily on to Bella's. Soon they were all hurtling down the slope shrieking with delight. Adam and Lenka were standing slightly awkwardly by our last sledge. Franz had the only other one. I noticed Janine had crept alongside him.

"You take this one," I urged Adam. I *did* owe him a favour for taking me down the mountain.

"You sure?"

"Absolutely."

They set off after the others, Lenka yelling with excitement as Adam expertly guided the sledge down the slope. Janine, Franz and I stood staring at each other. It was now or never. I took a deep breath. "Any chance of a ride on your sledge, Franz?"

"Sure! Let's go." He smiled happily at me and I felt my legs go weak.

"What about *me*?" Janine fumed. "I haven't got a sledge either."

Franz frowned at this dilemma. "Well, we can take turns, can't we?"

And so we did. Other people offered us rides on their sledges, but neither Janine or I were willing to give up going down with Franz. The feeling of his arms holding me tightly as we sped through the snow was too exciting. But as time went on there was still no shaking off Janine.

"She's like a limpet," I moaned to Georgia as I watched Janine walk back up the slope with Franz, giggling and flicking her hair.

"Is he acting like he's interested?" she asked.

"Not that I can tell. He's perfectly nice to both of us. I wish we could stay out here longer, but it's getting dark." I looked around; the lights of the village were coming on one by one and it was getting difficult to see where we were going.

"Why don't I ring Dad and ask if we can invite a few people back for hot chocolate?" Georgia suggested.

"Georgia, that's a brilliant idea! Then maybe I can get Franz to myself for a while."

Five minutes later it was all arranged and the grown-ups had agreed to stay in the kitchen and keep out of our way.

Gordon, Hamish and Ian had to go, but everyone else wanted to come, including Franz.

"Sure," he nodded. My heart skipped a beat.

"Great idea – thanks!" Janine gushed. My heart sank, but it would have been too rude to leave her out.

I walked back to the chalet with Georgia, our feet crunching in the thick snow. "Perhaps this wasn't such a good idea after all," I mumbled. "I reckon I'm still going to be fighting Janine for a chance to talk to Franz. If only we could find a way to keep her occupied – it's a pity there aren't any spare boys."

"I'll do what I can to help," said Georgia. "And what about asking Will and Adam to help keep her entertained."

"Are you mad! I don't want them to know I like Franz!" I hissed.

Georgia looked uncomfortable. "I think they might have guessed."

"How?"

"The sledge sharing for one … then there's the staring with the adoring eyes … the hanging on his every word…"

"It's not that obvious, is it?" I gasped.

"We-ell, there might be a *faint* possibility they haven't noticed. They are boys after all, but I wouldn't hold out much hope. Anyway, I'll do my best to help."

"Thanks," I whispered.

Georgia was right about Will and Adam. As soon as I sat down next to Franz, Will called over, "Oh, Emma, could you fetch Dizzy and Bella some crisps? You don't mind getting up, do you? I'm a bit busy looking after Marina..." I went to fetch the crisps, but when I came back I gave him a glare that said, "Don't you *dare* do that again." He smiled back, all innocent. I caught Adam watching Will, grinning. So he knew too. I found myself blushing. They were so *annoying*!

Eventually, everyone had a drink, crisps and dips and I had my place next to Franz on the sofa. I sank back, our shoulders almost touching, and smiled what I hoped was my most alluring smile.

"Hello. Who are you?" Nina was clambering up on to my lap in a pair of pink pyjamas.

"Nina!" I cried, but it was no good, she wasn't budging. She was staring at Franz with her piercing grey eyes.

"Are you in Emma's ski class?" she asked.

"No. I am in a ski class with Will and Adam," Franz answered politely.

"Do you have a girlfriend?"

"Nina!" I protested, horrified.

Franz shook his head. "No."

"Well, Emma and Georgia are both looking—"

"Isn't it time for you to go to bed now?" I cut Nina off as fast as I could.

"No, it isn't! Not for ages." She rolled her eyes at Franz, as if I was a lunatic, before continuing. "I have a boyfriend at school. He's called Deep. He says he's not, but he is really. And I *am* allowed other ones."

"I'm sure you have many boyfriends." Franz smiled.

"Not as many as Emma," Nina sighed. "She's had loads. But she's not had much luck here—"

"Nina!" I knew I had gone bright red, but she hadn't quite finished.

"And Georgia has never kissed a boy in her *life*. Never, ever, ever. But that's because she spends all her time with rocks."

I thanked my lucky stars that Georgia was sitting on the other side of the room, and Dizzy and Bella were too deep in conversation next to me to hear.

"*Nina!*" I gave a fake smile. "Why don't you go and talk to Will. He's got some exciting news. He's ... he's going to ask Marina to marry him," I finished wildly.

Her eyes widened. "Is he?"

I nodded solemnly.

"I could ask to be bridesmaid!" she gasped.

"You could!"

She slid on to the floor, wandered across the room and began chattering excitedly to Will and Marina. Marina started giggling. Will glared over at me. I smiled and gave him a little wave before turning back to Franz, who was looking mightily confused.

"Just a silly joke between me and Will. And don't listen to Nina, she's a bit crazy. *None* of that was true," I babbled, and then immediately thought how much cooler it would have been to have said nothing.

"Rocks?" Franz was frowning. "Rocks?"

So I spent my first proper conversation with my Austrian dream boy trying to explain about Georgia and her passion for rocks. And after that Janine came and joined us and I didn't manage to get a word in edgeways. She went on and on about what an amazing skier she was (a lie) and how luxurious her chalet was, and by then it was time for everyone to go home.

Dizzy and Bella said their goodbyes and set off into the icy night, pulling on their hats and gloves as it was

snowing hard again. Will had left earlier to walk a still giggling Marina home. Georgia was in the kitchen, and Janine had *finally* had to go to the loo, so it was just Adam, Lenka, Franz and me standing in the hallway.

There was a moment's awkwardness. I wondered if Adam was trying to pluck up the courage to ask Lenka out. I had looked up a few times during Janine's droning on and noticed him sitting by the fire, playing his guitar, and Lenka gazing up at him adoringly. I know he wasn't my Austrian dream boy, but I could see why Lenka found him attractive.

I was just trying to think of something to say when Lenka asked calmly, "Do you skate, Adam?" She pulled on a cute white hat. "I love skating."

"Er … I do skate actually…" Adam replied.

Lenka smiled flirtatiously. "Then why don't we go? The Christmas market will be here in a few days' time. People skate on the frozen lake. What do you think?"

"Sure," Adam nodded. "I'd love to."

"Good!" Lenka pulled her scarf round her neck and gave him a big smile. "See you tomorrow, everybody!"

And she disappeared into the night, leaving me, Adam and Franz staring politely at each other. I felt a bit deflated. How I wished I was as confident as Lenka. Why didn't I just say, "Franz, do you skate too?" But I just stared pointedly at him and hoped my expression was vaguely interested, but not completely desperate.

He opened his mouth to speak.

"Franz! Great, you haven't left yet!" Janine entered the hall like a whirlwind. "Would you mind walking me back to my chalet. It's not far. Thanks so much. And thank you all for a great evening!" She grabbed her coat and propelled Franz towards the door. He looked rather startled, but walked obediently out into the snow, thanking us as he went. Janine followed him, pushing the door firmly shut in our astonished faces.

I stared at Adam. "Did you see that! I mean, did you actually see that! I can't believe it! And stop laughing. It's all right for you, Mr Smug, you've got your date with Miss Slovakia."

Georgia appeared in the hall. "So?" She looked at us enquiringly. "Emma, what's the matter?"

"A terrible crime has just been committed," Adam said solemnly. "Janine's just stolen Franz from right under Emma's nose."

"This does mean, of course, that technically I've won the bet."

We were having breakfast the next morning. Adam was spooning large amounts of honey on to a hot roll, dripping with melted butter.

"No, it doesn't, Adam!" Georgia cried loyally. "Will got the first date, with Marina."

"Will's not going to marry Marina, Emma," Nina mumbled, looking up at me, her mouth full of toast. "You got that wrong. Marina says they're going to wait."

"Yeah. Thanks a bunch for that. Very funny." Will looked daggers across the table.

"Don't mention it."

"But," Adam stuck the spoon back in the jar, "getting back to my point, the bet was always between you and me, Emma. And that means I've won."

"Well, good for you," I said irritably.

"It wasn't fair play," Georgia said firmly. "Janine dragged Franz off before—"

"It was a stupid bet anyway," I snapped. "Can we just forget about it?"

I stared down at my cereal, willing them to change the subject.

I had hardly slept last night. I couldn't stop thinking about what might have happened between Franz and Janine on the walk home.

To make matters worse, there was no chance of seeing Franz this morning, as he was off visiting relatives.

I was going to see Janine, though, and I was dreading it.

"Well, I think you can stop worrying," Georgia said later, as we clattered gratefully into the warmth of the cable car, exhausted after our morning's boot camp with Gunter. "Franz obviously didn't ask her out."

I leaned against the window and grinned with relief. "I think you're right. If he *had* she would have arrived at ski school shouting the news through a

megaphone, whereas she's just been even more bad tempered than usual.

"Exactly." Georgia nodded. "So you can relax. Are you coming on the cross-country ski from the village to the frozen waterfall this afternoon? It's all on the flat, nothing scary. Dizzy and Bella are going. Apparently it's beautiful and the rock formations there are very interesting indeed…"

I gave her a sideways look and she grinned. "OK. Interesting for *me*."

I leaned over and gave her a big hug. "I love you and your rocks, Georgia. It's cool. But my bum is black and blue and I can't face putting on a pair of skis again, even on a flat surface, and … er…"

Georgia put on a schoolmistress face. "And?"

I tried not to look shifty. "And what?" I asked innocently.

"And I *know* Will mentioned that Franz would be back around lunchtime and therefore he might possibly be hanging around the village this afternoon," said Georgia.

"Did he? I don't remember."

I glanced at her and we burst out laughing.

"All right," I blushed. "I might have thought a stroll down to the village would be a nice idea. We both know that's what Janine will be doing. She practically sprinted out of the class just now. Franz must have told her his plans on their walk home last night. She's not going to give up on him yet."

Georgia nodded. "True. But is he really worth all this? Was he so wonderful when you talked to him yesterday?"

I hadn't told Georgia that most of my conversation with Franz had been about her. I couldn't possibly tell her what Nina had said about her never having kissed a boy. Georgia would have died of embarrassment. So I'd been very sparing on the details. But funnily enough, when I was talking to Franz about Georgia's interest in rocks, it had been the most relaxed I'd felt all night.

"I can't explain it," I sighed, "but he's the one. I know he is. Just imagine going back to school after Christmas and showing everyone my holiday photos, packed with the gorgeous Franz!"

Georgia frowned. "But what about *him*? You know, as a person. It's not just about what everyone else thinks! He's not a pin-up!"

I flushed. "No. Of course not. I know that. It's just that it would, er, make me feel better about something. He's the one I've dreamed about since…"

"Since what?"

The cable car stopped and everyone began to shuffle out.

"Since before I came out here." I looked at Georgia. "You see … there was this boy, Sam Harrison—"

"Georgia! Emma! Over here!" Dizzy and Bella were standing next to the cable car station and waving.

"Are you ready for the frozen waterfall?" shouted Bella.

Georgia waved back, before turning to me. "What about this Sam Harrison?"

I saw the girls walking towards us. "Never mind. I'll tell you another time. You go and have an amazing time with your rocks."

"I will! But we'll continue this later. Good luck this afternoon; I hope you find him."

I walked back to the chalet, dumped my stuff in the boot room and headed upstairs. I needed a bit of beautification before I hit the village. As I passed the sitting room I could hear someone laughing. I pushed open the door. Dad and Josie were playing cards, sitting at the little table where I had first seen Georgia and Adam.

Dad looked up. "Hi, Emma! I'm teaching Josie Hearts. Can you believe she's never played it?"

I caught Josie's eye.

No, I couldn't.

"Want to join us?" Dad asked enthusiastically.

"No thanks. I thought I'd go for a walk."

I thought I saw a look of relief cross Josie's face.

"OK," said Dad, "see you later. Have a good time."

I made a mental note that Will and I needed to talk about Dad at the next opportunity and hurried up to my room. I had a shower and washed my hair and then rifled through the wardrobe looking for the right thing to wear. At last I settled on a short black skirt, some black tights and a thin, long-sleeved, tight green T-shirt. I blow-dried my hair, put on some lipgloss, and a smudge of grey eye shadow and mascara. We were all tanned by now and my skin was glowing with all the sun and fresh air. As I went downstairs I noticed Adam's black ribbed sweater hanging on the banisters. I picked it up and held it against me – it felt soft and warm and it would have been perfect for keeping me warm, but he'd made such a fuss about Georgia borrowing it, I was pretty sure he'd go ballistic if he caught me in it.

I put it back – it wasn't right for meeting Franz in anyway. I wouldn't bother with a sweater at all, or a hat – it'd only spoil my carefully blow-dried hair. I'd be warm enough in my jacket. I looked at myself in the mirror and took a deep breath. I was ready.

Two hours later I wearily pushed open the sitting-room door. I was an iceberg. I'd walked back in a snowstorm and my hair and tights were wet through. Dad, Mrs Temple, Will and Nina were all playing cards, and Adam was sitting in one of the big armchairs quietly strumming his guitar.

Adam looked up. "Well, hello there! Don't tell me, the Drowned Rat look is really in this season. And may I congratulate you," he played a couple of chords, "because not many people can get away with it, but *you* have *totally* pulled it off."

I gave him a withering look. "Ha very ha."

Will stared at me. "Adam and I went to the pool

this afternoon, too. We must have missed you. Did you forget your swimming costume and go in fully clothed?"

Mrs Temple tutted loudly. "Just ignore them. I don't know what you've been up to, but I suggest you get upstairs and out of those wet things immediately."

Before I could escape, Nina piped up. "Mum and I were Christmas shopping and we saw you in the village," she said, fixing my dripping form with her clear, steady gaze. "You were all alone, sitting in the café. And when we had finished our shopping, you were in *another* café, *still* all on your own. Is that what being on 'Planet No Friends' means, because if it does, your friend Janine is on it too. She was sitting on her own in the window of the big hotel."

Adam raised his eyebrows at Will. They both understood what I'd been up to now. I blushed furiously. I knew I shouldn't have cared that Adam knew, but I did. I didn't want him to think I was a loser.

"Oh, poor Emma!" Will chortled. "Did you try *every* café in town looking for the beloved Franz?"

Adam grinned. "And did you bump into Janine doing the very same thing? Oh dear … one guy, two girls … someone's going to be disappointed…"

I looked away, feeling thoroughly beaten. I had just wasted a whole afternoon, all made up and in my nicest clothes, sitting all alone, for nothing. And now I would catch pneumonia and die.

"Emma, what are you still standing there for? You need to get out of those wet things," Mrs Temple said firmly. She was right. I needed to get upstairs and have a hot shower before I froze solid.

There was a banging of skis and poles being dropped downstairs in the boot room and the clatter of people coming upstairs. Then Georgia's face appeared round the sitting-room door. I could see she was flushed with excitement.

"Have a good time with the old rocks?" Adam asked.

"Great!" she replied. She looked at my bedraggled appearance anxiously. "Erm … I've brought some friends back for a hot chocolate, is that OK, Mum?"

"Of course," said Mrs Temple. "Don't keep them waiting in the hall, bring them in."

Lenka and Gordon came in first, followed by Franz.

Georgia flashed me a grin of triumph. I did the only

thing I could as I dripped like a melting snowman on to the floor. I gave him a weak smile.

Franz gave me a slightly puzzled look as he took in my appearance. "Hello, Emma. You should have come today. It was a great afternoon." He gave me one of his gorgeous shy grins.

"After you'd gone, we were waiting for the others on the road and we met Franz coming back in the car. He had his skis on the roof so he just hopped out and joined us," Georgia explained.

They then proceeded to tell me about what a wonderful time they'd had, and with every detail my smile became even more forced. Eventually I made an excuse and dashed upstairs. In double quick time, I changed my clothes, towel-dried my hair and hurried back down again – this was my chance to impress Franz with no Janine around to spoil things.

I sat down on the sofa next to Franz, but before I could even get a word out, Lenka flopped down next to me, smiling. "It's a shame you didn't come today, Emma. We missed you. We had so much fun, didn't we, Franz? And Adam and Will, why didn't you come? You can go to the pool any time." She shook her head at them. "So Emma, what did you get up to?"

Adam came over and squeezed in next to her. "Emma had some Christmas shopping to do this afternoon, didn't you?" He raised his eyebrows at me, and I managed a small smile of gratitude. Actually, I had bought one present, which I had been keeping dry under my coat, so it wasn't a total lie.

"I hope the weather gets better for skating," Lenka said, smiling flirtatiously at Adam.

"And for the Christmas market," Franz added. And suddenly, they all launched into a conversation about what it was going to be like, and in spite of my best efforts and glares at Adam, he wouldn't take the hint and whisk Lenka off to join in with Georgia and Gordon's conversation and leave Franz and me to talk alone.

After half an hour Lenka and Gordon said they had to go.

Adam and Georgia went with them into the hall to say goodbye. Will, who had now joined a heated game of Cheat with Nina, Dad and Mr and Mrs Temple, waved a farewell from the table.

Which left Franz and me alone on the sofa at last.

I looked up and smiled nervously. His beautiful green eyes were staring at me. I wondered if he could hear my heart thumping. It was now or never.

"Do you like pizza, Emma? Would you like to have a pizza with me?" He pushed a strand of hair out of his face.

"Er … yes," I squeaked. "I'd like that."

"Great. How about Friday – we can meet down in the village at seven."

"Perfect." I smiled up at him, feeling giddy with excitement.

Adam and Georgia came back into the room, and Franz jumped up. "I suppose I'd better get going too."

He said goodbye to everyone and I followed him into the hall.

"I'll see you then." He adjusted his scarf.

"Yes. See you," I said.

And he disappeared into the snowy darkness.

When the door closed after him I flattened my back against it and sank slowly to the floor, grinning from ear to ear.

Dreams do come true.

"What do you think is the longest time it has ever taken one person to learn to ski?" I leaned back in the hot tub and let the bubbles soothe my aching limbs. "Because I think I'm soon going to be qualifying for the *Guinness Book of Records*." I inspected some new bruises. "I don't think I can take another day."

"You say that every day, Emma," Adam sighed. He was sitting opposite me, next to Georgia and Nina. After the boys had discovered the pool yesterday, we had been keen to try it for ourselves after another hard day on the slopes. Will had already made plans to meet up with Marina, which was a pity as I still hadn't managed to talk to him about Dad and Josie.

"Pizza's not very romantic, is it?" Nina sighed, sinking briefly below the bubbles and resurfacing.

"We'd love to hear your opinion, Nina," Georgia sighed, "but thankfully Mum is calling you to go to the changing rooms with her."

Nina reluctantly clambered out of the hot tub. "It's so unfair," she grumbled. "I never get to hear the interesting conversations."

"Nina's right, though," Georgia said, after she'd gone. "It's a pity you're not going skating like Adam and Lenka, as there'd be loads of opportunity for Franz to pick you up when you fall, which could be kind of romantic..."

"Oh, yes," Adam agreed. "Loads. It's hard to imagine quite how many of those opportunities there would be."

I kicked him under the bubbling water. "OK, so maybe I'm not the most brilliant skier in the world. Stop laughing. But I bet I *could* skate, Mr Smartypants. I bet I'd be good. I bet skating with me would be like..."

"Dragging a sack of potatoes across the ice?"

I lunged forward and splashed as much water as I could in his face. He gave me a pitying "is that the best you can do" look, ducked down and grabbed my ankles. I disappeared underwater. After a few seconds I resurfaced, coughing and spluttering.

"Stop it, you two!" Georgia yelled. "And Adam, leave Emma alone." She rolled her eyes at me. "God, brothers are such a pain, aren't they?"

I nodded.

"You excited, though?" she asked.

"Yes, of course," I replied with a bright smile.

But there was something the matter. I knew there was because deep down I felt terrified. When Franz had first asked me out I was the happiest girl in the world, but now hundreds of doubts and worries had begun to set in. The day after tomorrow I was going out with the best-looking boy ever, and all I could think about was my disastrous date with Sam Harrison. What if I made a complete mess of it? Again. What if I was the kind of girl boys simply didn't find interesting to talk to? I had to get it right this time. This date *had* to be perfect.

Georgia was staring at me, frowning. "Emma? What's up? You're not nervous, are you?"

"Nooo." I shook my head.

Georgia gave a disbelieving snort. "You are! But *why*? Franz is lovely and he's so easy to talk to – we never stopped yakking on the waterfall trip. And you've been on loads of dates before, haven't you?"

I looked across at Adam. I really didn't want him to hear this, but I couldn't keep avoiding the truth. I took a deep breath and screwed up my face. "One."

"You *see* … what did I tell you—" She did a double take. "What?! How many?"

"One. And it was a disaster."

"Skiing date, was it?" Adam asked drily.

"Very funny," I snapped.

"Shut up, Adam," Georgia cried. "*Your* last date was hardly a roaring success, was it?"

Adam flushed. "What do you know about that?"

"Hattie's sister knows Evon's brother and he does judo with my friend Nellie."

"Oh, terrific. Good to know I'm at the top of the gossip list. Anyway, I don't care. I've been on enough dates to know that sometimes they just don't work out."

"Yes, but *why* didn't your date with Hattie work out, Adam?" Georgia's brows furrowed. "Was it some fatal flaw in your dating technique? And what if you make the same mistake again with Lenka?"

Georgia tut-tutted and shook her head.

"Leave it out, Little Miss Confidence-Booster!" Adam protested. "I don't need advice from someone who has never even *been* on a date. I'll be fine, thank you very much."

"But will you?" Georgia ploughed on. "Just imagine the misery and shame if it goes wrong again…"

"Stop talking about disastrous dates!" I yelled at her. "You're terrifying me. This date with Franz has to go well, it just *has* to."

"So what went wrong on your one and only other date, then?" Adam asked.

I shrugged. "I don't know. Apart from pretending I was interested in football to get it in the first place. That was a pretty big mistake. But there are a million other things to talk about, aren't there? That's the thing – I really and truly would like to know anything I could have done to have made it go better. It's not like you get a report on a date and marks out of ten, is it?"

"'Conversation – lost the will to live; Appearance – can be a bit wet and shivery at times…' That kind of thing?" Adam suggested, grinning.

"Mmm. That kind of thing," I nodded. "Something like, 'Personality – thinks he's funny but is totally deluded.'"

Georgia giggled.

"But seriously," I went on, "if you did get marks out of ten, at least you'd know what went wrong. If only

I could work out what I need to do to make me the perfect date *before* I go out with Franz..."

Georgia sat up. "Well, the solution's obvious. For both of you," she cried. "You need a practice date."

"A what?" Adam and I chorused.

"A practice date. You and Adam go out for an evening. Erm ... it'll have to be tomorrow and you'll have to be horribly honest with each other. I'll work out the categories. By the time you both go out with your real dates you'll know exactly what to do and nothing could possibly go wrong..."

There was an awkward silence. Then Adam said slowly, "OK, I'll do it, but only as a favour to Emma, because let's face it, she's going to need all the help she can get." I kicked him again.

"And I'll do it because I really, really like Lenka and you don't stand a chance of a second date after she's spent some time alone with you."

"Charmed, I'm sure." Adam grinned.

"OK then." Georgia took a deep breath. "The rules are this – it has to be just like a real date and as far as possible you must do what you are going to do on your real dates. That way you'll both be ready for any potential pitfalls and disasters!"

"But I'm going skating," Adam protested.

"And I'm going for a pizza..."

Georgia gave an exasperated snort. "Well, you'll have to go skating for a bit and then go for a pizza."

"God no," Adam wailed. "Not skating – there's no way I'm spending any time on ice with Bambi here."

"Being *rude* is *not* the same as being honest, is it, Georgia?" I complained.

"Be quiet, both of you. Now listen, here are the categories you're going to mark each other on." Georgia ticked them off her fingers:

"Appearance; Interesting conversation; Sense of humour and ... Kissing ability!"

"Whoa!" Adam and I howled in embarrassment.

Georgia grinned. "Well, skip *that*, obviously. But you must be totally honest with each other about the other categories. You mustn't spare each other's feelings."

"Agreed," we chorused.

Georgia looked pleased with herself. "Well, that's that then. Sorted. Practice date starts at 6.30pm tomorrow. Number One Category: Appearance. First impressions matter, you know..."

How much effort do you make on a practice date?

It felt really weird trying to look as nice as I possibly could for *Adam*.

"It's not for Adam, though, is it?" Georgia explained, sitting on my bed and swinging her legs. "It's testing out the look you're going to go for on your date with *Franz* the dreamy."

"But what if Franz and Adam like different things?"

Georgia sighed. "They won't. Boys aren't that complicated."

"Oh, really? And what about *you*, Georgia? You're very happy to help me get a date, but we still haven't fixed you up. Are you sure Gordon isn't the one – he seems to really like you."

One quick glance in her direction told me to change the subject. "OK, OK, I promise not to mention him again. But what about the boy at the pool yesterday *and* the French boy at the restaurant today?"

She smiled and shrugged her shoulders. I knew she'd never admit it, but recently Georgia had begun to get quite a lot of attention.

"I mean, look at you, Georgia…" I went on. "You're gorgeous. The boys are noticing *you*, that's for sure. When are you going to notice one of *them*?"

"I told you. I'll know when the right boy for me comes along. OK, how are you doing?" she asked, swiftly changing the subject. "That eye shadow looks great on you; I think I'll give it a try too."

Out of the corner of my eye I saw Will walking past our room.

"Hang on, I'll be back in a second."

I dashed out on to the landing. "Will!" I hissed. "Will, hold on a minute, I need to talk to you."

He stopped and frowned. "You're not going to ask me for brotherly advice about your practice date, are you? Georgia's got to be mad! You and Adam? You'll kill each other before the end of the evening."

"No. It's not about that. Listen, I'm worried about Dad."

Will looked at me. "In what way?" he asked.

"In the Josie-all-over-him-all-the-time way," I replied.

"I know you're going to laugh, but I seriously think she's after him. She's so adoring towards him. And I'm worried she's using him, too. She knows he's got loads of connections and she's desperate to get on as a writer herself."

Will looked uncomfortable. "Actually, I think you might be right. Ever since Dad broke his ankle, she's not let him out of her sight. She's turned into a real little Florence Nightingale."

"What do you think Dad thinks of *her*?"

"I'm not sure he's really noticed. I mean, I'm sure he likes her and everything – how could he not when she's making such an effort? But whether he thinks of her, you know … like that, I'm not sure."

"Well, the next time we get Dad alone, I think it's time for a few searching questions, don't you?"

Will nodded. "OK." He jerked his head in the direction of my room. "Better be getting back to your pre-date preparations. I've told Adam to be really brutal. It's the only way you'll learn."

"Thanks, Will, you're so thoughtful."

"You're welcome. Have a good evening. I'm off to meet someone," he said vaguely. "See you later."

I hurried back into the bedroom.

"Well, you can't do that tomorrow," Georgia sighed, handing me my date notebook. "You wouldn't waste beautification time chatting if it was Franz you were seeing tonight, would you?"

I gave my hair a final brush. "I suppose not."

"No suppose about it. Now are you ready?" And I was. Skinny black jeans, black boots, and my soft grey sweater over a pretty white lacy shirt. I quickly finished off with some mascara and a slick of eyeliner.

Georgia nodded. "Very nice. Now let's go and see what Adam's wearing."

We hurried downstairs. Dad was sitting on the sofa, reading. Nina and Mr Temple were playing Scissors Paper Stone next to him. Josie and Mrs Temple were in the kitchen.

Adam was standing in front of the fire. "Don't say a word," he said grumpily. "Nina's already told me this shirt is completely wrong." He gave it a tug.

"Ah, Adam," his dad grinned, "and so it begins. A lifetime of being bossed around by women..."

Nina stopped her game and raised her eyebrows meaningfully at me.

"She's right, Adam." I nodded. "You looked much better in the grey one you were wearing the other night."

"I told you!" said Nina triumphantly. "Makes your eyes look nice."

"*How?*" Adam asked, bewildered.

"More grey," I said firmly. "Much better, honestly. But the jeans are good. What about me, Nina?"

"Good," she replied. "What do you think, Adam?"

"Yes, what d'you think, Adam?" Mr Temple echoed.

"Can we have some help in the kitchen, please?" Mrs Temple was standing in the doorway, looking meaningfully at Dad and Mr Temple. "*Now.*" After a few reluctant grumbles, they did as they were told. Mrs Temple smiled back at Adam and me. "Now, you two won't be here for supper and neither will Will. What are you up to, Georgia?"

"I'm meeting Dizzy and the others."

"My, my, what a hectic social life you all have. Well, I hope you all have a good time." She disappeared back into the kitchen to supervise the dads.

"So," I asked, turning back to Adam. "How *do* I look?"

He looked me up and down, and pulled a face. "We-ell, at least you tried."

"Adam!" I yelled. "You're not being helpful at all. Stop mucking about. Now, seriously, would you change anything?" I gave a twirl.

He looked again. "Not really, you look fine."

"Fine? Noooo!" Mr Temple yelled from behind the kitchen door. This was swiftly followed by the sound of Dad laughing before some sharp words from Mrs Temple shut them up.

"*Fine?* What's *that* supposed to mean?" I said.

"It means you look fine."

"Can't you do better than that?"

Adam put his head in his hands and groaned. "That's enough! You're doing my head in already, and we haven't even got out of the door yet." He took a deep breath. "But I know it will be different tomorrow."

"Why's that?" I asked.

"You're nuts and Lenka isn't."

"Adam," I said firmly, "Lenka is a *girl*. And if you want to know what girls like, you've got to stop fooling about and listen to me, OK?"

"Yes, Miss." He grinned.

"Have you got your notebook?"

"Yes, Miss." He held it out for inspection.

I frowned at him. "Come on, then." I went into the hall, pulled on my coat and stuck the notebook Georgia had given me in my pocket. "Let's get this over with."

I could hear Georgia and Nina giggling in the sitting room. "Bye!" called Georgia. "Have a good time, and remember, I want a full report as soon as you get back!"

We began at the ice rink. For all my big talk in the hot tub the day before, I was dreading it. And with good reason. I simply couldn't stay on my feet. Whoever had the great idea that trying to balance on two blades of steel might be fun was a lunatic. My behind was so frequently in contact with the ice that an attractive damp patch soon appeared on the back of my jeans. After half an hour I begged for mercy and we took a well-earned rest.

"I have an official complaint," Adam gasped, leaning on the side of the rink. "This is not a faithful recreation of what is going to happen tomorrow. Tomorrow I will be skating with Lenka, who no doubt will be an Olympic-standard skater. You, on the other hand, are rubbish…"

"Oh, that's nice. That's very nice indeed." I got out my notebook. "I'm writing 'hurtful and cruel' here."

"I'm writing 'skates like Bambi on ice' here." He pulled his pencil out of his coat pocket. "AND ... 'doesn't make any effort when you try to pull her up off the ice, but lies there, as I predicted, like a sack of potatoes'."

I gave him a look and began to write again. "'Not very strong...'" I muttered under my breath.

"Not very strong! Rambo would be losing his strength after picking you up the number of times I've had to..."

I stared at him over my notebook before scribbling my next comment. Adam peered over my shoulder. "*Whiney!*" he cried, and burst out laughing. "That's so unfair! I was going on to say that it's also not a truthful recreation as we are on an ice rink and *not* on the frozen lake surrounded by the twinkling stalls of the Christmas market."

I looked around. "True, it's hardly very romantic, but then you're not a very romantic person, are you, Adam?"

"Yes, I am!" he cried. There was a pause. "*Why* aren't I?"

"Let's go and get a pizza and I'll tell you." We handed in our skates and I gratefully slipped my feet back into my boots. We walked through the village, which seemed even more magical at night with all the fairy lights twinkling away, and made our way to the pizza restaurant.

We took a table in the window, and after some debate about which was the best pizza topping, ordered our food.

Adam looked around. "So this is where it'll all be happening tomorrow night. I can just see it now ... the gorgeous Franz feeding you a slice of pepperoni pizza across the table ... yuck! But enough about your date. Let's talk about me. Tell me why I'm not romantic..."

"One word, Adam. 'Compliments.' None. Not one so far. You've got to say nice things to a girl."

"Like what?"

"Like 'You've got lovely eyes' or 'I like the way you laugh' or 'You're a great skater'." I flashed him a look. "Don't say a word, Adam, I'm not talking about me ... it's Lenka you're going out with. You can hardly be stuck for nice things to say about her, can you? Do you think I should compliment Franz?"

"What? Tell *him* he's got beautiful eyes?"

"Well, he has," I protested.

"No. He'll think you're weird. What else do you like about him, apart from his appearance?"

I had a think. "Georgia says he's really easy to talk to."

"Georgia! What about you?"

I bit my lip. "I've only spoken to him a bit. Actually, that's the thing I'm most anxious about. I'm worried I won't be able to think of anything to say. That's what happened before."

"That's pretty hard to imagine. I've had to write 'talks too much' more than once in the last hour." He got out his notebook and pretended to read. "'Never stops' ... blah blah blah blah blah ... and oh yes, last entry, 'Tragically, thinks she's interesting...'"

I grinned. "Stop it, I know you won't believe me, but it really did happen and I'm terrified it will happen again. All Sam wanted to talk about was football and I knew nothing about it."

"Didn't he try and talk about anything else?"

"No, and I couldn't think of anything, either. We just sat there in silence – it was really awkward."

"Sounds like you just didn't have anything in common, but I do know what you mean. My last date was a bit like that, too."

"But it won't be like that tomorrow. Lenka's really easy to talk to."

Adam nodded. "She is, isn't she? But according to Georgia, so is Franz, so you shouldn't have anything to worry about, either."

We were both silent for a moment, but then our pizzas arrived and we got sidetracked into talking about our favourite toppings again, which somehow turned into talking about our friends and then somehow we got back to pizzas, and the most disgusting toppings we could imagine. By the time we realized that was not going to be a suitable subject for conversation for our real dates, the waitress had arrived with the dessert menu. Adam ordered the cheesecake, but as this was my practice date, and I didn't want Franz thinking I was a greedy pig, I regrettably shook my head.

"Not for me, thanks." The waitress disappeared and returned a few minutes later with a delicious-looking chocolate cheesecake. Adam began to tuck in.

"So," I said, eyeing his pudding, "how do you think it's going so far? How am I doing?"

Adam watched as I helped myself to his cheesecake. "If you leave Franz's dessert alone it might be just about OK. What about Lenka? How am I doing?"

I was about to reply when a familiar voice cut in. "Didn't think I'd be seeing *you* two out together the night before your big dates … sharing pudding, too. How romantic. Has someone not told me something?"

We looked up. Janine was staring down at us. I had told Dizzy and Bella about Franz during ski school this morning and word had obviously got round...

"Erm…" I said, giving Adam a desperate look.

"Dates are very much on," said Adam hastily. "Emma and I just fancied a pizza, that's all."

"Well, it all looks very cosy to me. My mom and I have been sitting over there for ages and you're both so busy chatting you never even noticed we were here…"

There was an awkward pause. Then Adam looked up and gazed at Janine with an intense stare.

"Has anyone ever told you that you have *really* beautiful hair…" His eyes locked on to hers and he smiled. "It's such a *lovely* colour."

My mouth dropped open.

Janine blushed the colour of beetroot. "Wow, thanks, Adam." She beamed at him, then she remembered I was there and her face clouded over. "It's a shame that someone else won't get a chance to appreciate it as much as you do." She sniffed and gave me a pointed look. "Right, I'd better be getting back. See you, *Adam*."

"What did you do that for?" I hissed, as Janine returned to her table.

Adam grinned. "I was practising my compliments. And if I do say so myself, 'RESULT'. Thanks, Emma."

"You can't compliment *her*," I said, ignoring his advice and stealing another spoonful of cheesecake.

He frowned. "Why not?"

"Because!" I said. "And what are you writing now?"

"'Quite spiteful towards other girls.'"

"No, I'm not! But a tip for when you're on your date with Lenka – don't go round telling other girls that they have beautiful hair. She won't be impressed."

"Okey-dokey. Point taken. But it wasn't so much a compliment as a diversion tactic … to stop her getting ideas about us. The last thing we need is Janine getting the wrong end of the stick and spreading rumours."

"You and me?" I laughed. "As if! But seriously, Adam. Do you think it's going to be OK with Franz tomorrow?"

"If you would only listen to my advice," he said, batting my spoon away from his plate. "And do you think it's going to be OK with Lenka?"

"How can it not be? She's great. She's beautiful, kind, interesting..."

"Do *you* want to go out with her, then?"

I ignored him. "You *have* been a tiny bit helpful, actually," I said. "I know now not to ask a boy's opinion on anything to do with my appearance and not to say I don't want a dessert and then eat his."

"Very good. I don't see how you can go wrong. And I've learned I must say nice things to my date, but never, ever to anyone else."

"Excellent."

He looked across the table at me and raised his Coke bottle.

"Good luck to us, then."

"Good luck to us," I agreed.

We clinked bottles and I crossed my fingers for tomorrow night.

Twenty-four hours later I was sitting at the same table in the same pizza restaurant. Except instead of Adam sitting opposite me, it was Franz.

And it wasn't going quite as well as I had hoped. In fact it was shaping up to be the Sam Harrison experience all over again. After my practice date, I hadn't felt that nervous about going out with Franz. In fact, it was a bit weird how not nervous I was, considering how much time I'd spent fantasizing about it. Me, Emma Delamare, had got a date with the most gorgeous boy in the ski resort, just like I had dreamed I would.

I replayed the evening so far…

Franz had come to pick me up at 7pm, as agreed. Georgia answered the door and left him standing outside, while she ran behind the sitting-room door, rolled her eyes and pretended to faint.

"You're right, he is a god," she swooned. And there was no denying it. In his big black ski jacket and huge green scarf that matched his eyes, he did look totally gorgeous.

"Hello," I said shyly, as I came into the hall and collected my coat off the peg.

"Hello," he answered.

I crossed my fingers that the level of conversation was going to improve as the evening went on.

Adam had appeared in the hall, hastily zipping up his coat. Against my wishes, he was going to walk with us down into the village, where he was meeting Lenka.

"Do you *have* to come with us?" I whispered as we set off down the path.

He raised his eyebrows. "Well, I could walk a few steps behind if you'd rather, but my date happens to be now-ish too. Plus, I'm saving you from yourself."

"*You're what?*"

"I just know you're not going to be able to resist doing something creepy like telling him he's got lovely shiny hair or something weird like that."

I elbowed him hard and he staggered sideways in the snow, chuckling to himself.

The market traders had been setting up their stalls all day. As we'd neared the village you could smell the cinnamon in the mulled wine and the spicy tang of gingerbread and plum cakes mixed with the scent of pine cones and candle wax. Hundreds of Christmas decorations hung all around us. There were brightly-coloured wooden Christmas figures, gold ornaments, delicate glass baubles and silver angels blowing trumpets that chimed as they flew. In the village square an old-fashioned painted merry-go-round carrying smiling children sitting on fat wooden horses turned to the sound of an organ. We soon spotted Lenka in the crowd. She was wearing her little white hat with matching short jacket, short skating skirt and white tights tucked into a pair of long boots. She looked absolutely stunning. However long I spent getting ready for a date, I'd never look like that … I wondered if Adam was feeling nervous as I watched him make his way through the crowd towards her…

"Emma? Emma? Did you hear me?"

I turned back to Franz and the pizza restaurant with a start. "I'm sorry," I gasped. "What were you saying? Something about giga-whatsits?"

He nodded. "At school we're making a computer that can communicate with people all over the world. We're very lucky that in my school we have the technology to do it…"

"Wow," I said feigning enthusiam. "Tell me more."

I put my elbows on the table and propped my head in my hands. I hoped it wasn't going to be anything like the last story about what hilarious fun they had making a walkie-talkie and the jokes they played on the maths teacher with it. It's not that Franz wasn't funny, it's just that his sense of humour was different to mine. I gave myself a shake. I absolutely had to make a success of this evening. I would concentrate on gazing into his gorgeous eyes. As long as I kept focused, everything would be fine.

But however hard I tried I just couldn't seem to relax and let myself get caught up in the evening.

I wondered if it was the venue. Nina was right – a pizza restaurant wasn't really that romantic, not compared to skating on a frozen lake with a beautiful Christmas market going on in the background. Maybe Franz and I should have gone there. But then I remembered what Adam had said about my skating and smiled. I would have been rubbish. But it might have been more fun than this…

"What do you like to do?" Franz asked after he had finished his story. This was how our conversation had gone, politely taking turns, no interruptions and no teasing.

I thought about the question. Adam had said to be totally open and honest with Franz about myself, so I replied, "Writing. I like to write."

"That's good. What do you write?"

"Stories, mostly."

"About what?"

"Erm … about people, and their friends and what they get up to … you know, dramas in people's lives, that kind of thing. I want to be a writer when I'm older, like my dad."

Franz nodded, obviously struggling for something else to say. "I want to be an inventor."

"What do you want to invent?" I asked.

"A machine to make our pizzas get cooked faster." He chortled at his joke.

I creased my face up into a smile and pretended to laugh.

There was no doubt at all that Franz was a really nice person – Georgia was right about that, and I knew I owed her big time because she'd talked about me loads to get his interest. So maybe it was me who turned dates flat and into hard work, because, just like my date with Sam, I was staring across a table at a fantastic-looking boy and I couldn't feel any kind of spark between us.

What was wrong with me? He was so gorgeous. Why oh why wasn't this date easy and fun? I wanted it to work so badly, but we just didn't seem to be on the same wavelength.

After we had eaten we walked in silence back down through the village and into the Christmas market. I looked out for Adam and Lenka, but they were nowhere to be seen.

As we wandered up through the little wood to the chalet I felt the tension rising. Would Franz try and kiss me? When we got to the front door we stood, embarrassed for a moment, then he leaned forward, smiled awkwardly and planted his lips on mine. I closed my eyes. Surely this was going to be "dreamy" and "thrilling" just like I'd hoped… But it wasn't. It wasn't unpleasant, but exciting? Let's just say after a moment I opened my eyes and started looking around. And that's when I spotted Adam and Lenka wandering up the path to the chalet. I leaped away.

"Thanks, Franz. That was a lovely evening," I said loudly.

"I enjoyed it too. Thanks…"

Adam and Lenka were nearly at the door. What if they wanted to have a goodnight kiss? I needed to get out of here.

I pushed the door open. "Bye then…"

"Maybe we see each other…?" Franz asked.

"Absolutely … there's no ski school tomorrow, and we're going on a family outing with the Temples, so maybe the day after?"

Franz nodded.

"OK. Bye then…" I hurried inside and shut the door. I heard Franz saying his goodbyes to Adam and Lenka and his footsteps crunching away. I needed to get out of the hall. I didn't want to hear the silence that would tell me that Adam and Lenka were kissing, or to talk to Adam about our dates when he got in. But before I could escape, Georgia appeared from the sitting room.

"Parents all over the place in there, let's go up to our room," she said, dragging me upstairs.

"Is that you, Emma?" Dad called out. I yelled back that I'd be down in a minute.

"So how was it?" Georgia whispered as we climbed the stairs. "I want to know everything. You missed a vicious ping-pong tournament with the others. I think Janine was pretending the ping-pong ball was you."

"Any new boys there?" I asked, giving her a look.

"A couple."

"At least one of them interested in you, I bet?"

She flushed. "Might have been."

"Any chance you were interested in them?"

She grinned at me sheepishly and shook her head. "I can't help it, Emma! I can't *force* myself to like someone in that way! Now don't change the subject. How did it go?" She sat down on her bed expectantly.

"It was great. Really great," I lied.

"He lived up to expectations, then?"

"Absolutely." I flopped down on my bed.

"He *is* great company, isn't he?"

"The best," I said, trying to sound excited. "We got on like a house on fire. It was fantastic."

"And did you have a goodnight kiss?"

I nodded.

"And was it complete and total heaven?"

Fortunately, I was stopped from reliving our "heavenly" kiss by the sound of the front door closing. Adam bounded up the stairs and stuck his head round our door, his hair all tousled.

He smiled at me. "Well, Emma, no need to ask you if your date was OK."

"It was more than 'OK'," Georgia snorted. "Sounds to me as if Emma had Franz *totally* under her spell."

"Did she?" Adam raised an eyebrow. "Well, that's good."

"She was in the middle of telling me all about it, but perhaps we should hear how your date with the gorgeous Lenka went as well?"

"Actually, guys," I said desperately, "I promised Dad I'd go down and say goodnight, and to be honest, I'm totally exhausted. Must be all the excitement. Can it wait till tomorrow?"

And I dashed past their surprised faces and ran downstairs.

"So, come on, Adam, how did it go?" Georgia asked, stretching over the table to grab another croissant.

Adam had just taken a mouthful of cereal. He nodded. "Mmm ... great."

I felt depressed.

I had lain awake most of the night wondering what on earth was the matter with me. Not one, but now *two* gorgeous boys had asked me out, and each time had been a disaster. At least Franz hadn't dumped me yet. But I had to admit that I wasn't exactly jumping with joy to see him again. The whole evening had been such a strain and I really wasn't looking foward to seeing him after ski school tomorrow, with all our friends looking on and listening. I sighed with relief that I didn't have to face that today. Natalie and Parisa had been right all along – personality did count. A lot. And even though Franz was drop-dead gorgeous *and* I knew he was a nice person, we just hadn't clicked.

I could see from Georgia's face that she was bursting with more questions for me so I was glad of the distraction when Nina made her way round the breakfast table, solemnly placing a handwritten list in front of each of us.

"What's this?" Adam asked, picking it up.

Nina sighed. "My Christmas list. There's only a few days to go and no one's asked me what I want yet, except Mum and Dad." She glared at them. "And they're not giving me what I *really* want..."

"A white pony with a black star on its forehead," Adam read. He leaned forward and raised his eyebrows at his parents, who were sitting with Dad at the end of the table. "Mmm ... OK, Nina, let's see, what shall I get you ... the pony... Why not? Oh no, look, *much* better ... a sparkly *pink pen*."

Nina fixed him with one of her coolest looks.

"Don't tease her," his mum called down the table.

"A purple four-poster bed," Georgia began to read her copy. "A white piano, a pair of see-through glitter shops..."

"Shoes," Nina corrected her firmly. "With high heels. And ankle straps."

"A Pop Princess doll, a Pop Princess outfit, a *karaoke* machine? A small *stage*?"

Nina nodded. "I'm thinking of starting a band."

"Nina's going to sing at the talent contest at the Christmas Party," said Mrs Temple proudly. The biggest hotel in the village was having a Christmas Eve party and everyone seemed to be going, including us.

Georgia groaned. "No, Mum, no, please don't let her do it. She loves the limelight so much, it can't be good to indulge her."

"Well, we're all supposed to do something, if we can," said Dad. He swirled his hands around in front of him. "I shall be doing my magic tricks."

Will put his head in his hands. "Nooo, please don't let him do it. He loves the limelight so much, it can't be good to indulge him."

"I bet you're wonderful," Josie beamed at Dad.

Will and I exchanged a look across the table.

After breakfast we were sent upstairs to put on some more layers of clothing. The Temples had arranged for us all to go on a sleigh ride to the next village, where we were going to have lunch. I was looking forward to it. It would be a relief to be with just Will, Dad and the Temples. I could relax and have some fun.

Five minutes later we were all back in the sitting room ready to go when there was a knock at the front door. "Who's that?" Will asked. "Surely not Father Christmas coming early with a purple four-poster bed. Or is it the white pony?"

Nina stuck out her tongue at him.

"It's Lenka," Adam replied, heading for the hall. "She asked if there was a spare place on our sleigh today and there was, so I invited her along."

"Great," I smiled, but inside I felt disappointed. It would have been nice to have a day without anyone else. Then Lenka appeared and I felt guilty because she was so sweet and friendly to everyone. Just because my date hadn't gone well, that was no reason for me to feel grumpy that Adam's had.

We piled out of the chalet, with Josie running after us with instructions for looking after Dad's ankle. The sleighs set off from the main square in the village and we could hear the tinkling of the bells on the horses' harnesses as we approached. The sun was shining, but it was going to be cold.

The Temples and Lenka all piled into the big sleigh, and Will, Dad and I shared a smaller one. Dad tucked the thick blankets round me as we got ready to set off.

"You all right?" he asked, pulling a face at me.

"Sure," I smiled. The driver made a clicking sound and the sleigh lurched off.

"Date with Mr Wonderful go OK last night? You've been very quiet about it."

"It was brilliant, thanks."

"Why brilliant?" Will asked.

I shrugged. "You know, just brilliant."

"You don't sound that convinced."

"I am convinced! And anyway, what do you know about being convinced? You change girlfriends more frequently than you change your socks. I'd only just got to know Marina, but I gather you were out with *another* girl last night. I thought you seemed a bit vague about where you were going. So Marina's been dumped? Adam said the new lucky lady is French..."

"Swiss," Will corrected me.

"Well, whoever she is, I really feel that I should warn her about you. I hope you're not going to dump her after just two dates, too?"

Will screwed up his face. "I can't promise … there's a lovely Irish girl who I met in the queue for the cable car yesterday…"

"For goodness' sake, Will! What are you playing at?"

"I'm searching for the right one."

"Pretty thorough search," I snorted, staring out at the last buildings of the village as the sleigh glided along the road.

"And how will you know when you've met the right one?" asked Dad.

Will shrugged. "I'll just know."

Dad leaned forward and his face became serious.

"How would you feel if … if … I thought I'd met someone special?"

Will and I stared at each other in horror.

"I don't think you're ready, Dad," I replied at once. "I think that you'd be making a terrible mistake. It's much too soon after Mum…"

"It's over two years!" Dad exclaimed. "And I know you've had to look after yourselves a lot since your mum and I split up. Wouldn't it be nice to have someone else around who was good at looking after people?"

I looked down at his plastered foot. Josie had found a special plastic covering to keep it dry.

"No! We're fine just as we are, Dad." Will looked desperate. "Aren't we, Emma? I think we'd find it very hard getting used to a new person. It's all been very stressful with you and Mum and we're still sort of dealing with that, aren't we?"

I nodded vigorously. "We really are, Dad. Please, please don't make any decisions just yet. You don't want to do something you might regret."

"I don't think I would..." He looked at both our faces and sat back in the sleigh with a sad smile. "OK. Let's leave it for the moment then, shall we?"

Will and I stared at each other, half relieved, half guilty. Dad did look really unhappy, but we were saving him from making a huge mistake. The thought of Josie entering our lives on a permanent basis was too awful to contemplate. Why couldn't Dad see how fake she was? He was normally such a good judge of character. But Josie was young and adoring, so who could blame him for being taken in?

"Where's Franz today?" Will asked, changing the subject. "You could have brought him along."

"I didn't know that we were inviting other people," I said crisply. "I thought it was family only."

"Oooh," Will teased, "am I sensing a bit of jealousy? Adam's girlfriend is here, your boyfriend isn't."

"Don't be ridiculous!" I sniffed, but I was furious to feel myself blushing.

"Ooh, I'm right, aren't I? You're annoyed Franz isn't here too, aren't you? But if you had such a great date last night, I don't understand why you didn't just ask if there was some space on the ride, like Adam did. That shows keenness to me. Perhaps you didn't really want Franz to come. Maybe the date wasn't that good after all?"

I knew Will was only mucking about, but I wasn't enjoying it.

"Franz and I had a great time, thank you. In fact it was a really romantic evening, which is something you wouldn't know anything about, Will."

"Ouch, so cutting," Will chortled. "Well, at least it wasn't another Sam Harrison disaster. I couldn't stand any more of your grumpiness, though to be honest you seem quite touchy today considering it went so well. So the practice date worked for both of you, did it?"

I nodded, wrapped the blankets closer around me and joined Dad in watching the stream tumble down under the snow-covered rocks as the horses trotted across a wooden bridge.

We ate lunch in an old-fashioned chalet in a tiny hamlet. I was grateful for the cosy warmth of the huge fire as we stepped inside and found our table – even with the blankets it had been a chilly ride. Will, Nina and I sat opposite Lenka, Adam and Georgia. Dad and Mr and Mrs Temple were now well trained at keeping themselves to themselves at the other end of the table.

"Lenka's so pretty, isn't she?" Nina whispered to me, as we looked at the menus.

I looked over at Lenka laughing with Adam. Her eyes were sparkling, and as she talked, she flicked her long blonde hair over her shoulder.

"Yes, she is," I nodded.

"I think Adam's really lucky, don't you?"

"Yes, I do." I stared at my menu. Across the table Lenka was placing Adam's hands on her face so he could feel how cold it was.

What was the matter with me? Why couldn't Franz and I be like that? I had to work out what was going wrong.

"Emma? Emma?" Georgia was trying to attract my attention. "You're miles away – what are you thinking about? Or can I guess?" She gave me a meaningful smile.

The others were all looking at me now.

"She was dreaming about Franz, of course," Nina said cheerfully. "Weren't you?"

I felt myself blush.

"See," Nina nodded smugly. "I told you. You were, weren't you?"

I looked up straight into Adam's grey eyes, which were staring at me enquiringly, like the others. With a huge effort, I managed to throw my brightest smile around the table.

"That's for me to know!" I laughed. "Come on, who else is going to have the pancakes?"

After lunch we walked up a small road until we got to a tiny white church up above the village. An old stone well had been built into the rock next to it and a smiling

Austrian family were throwing coins into the water. Dad explained that local people believed it would grant you a wish.

"Let's all have a wish then!" Nina cried eagerly. "Come on you two slowcoaches!" she yelled back at Lenka and Adam, who were lagging behind, giggling. Hearing Lenka's laugh had made me realize all the more how I should be feeling about Franz. But I wasn't.

"OK!" Georgia laughed. "You never know ... they may come true."

On the way home Nina wanted to try the small sleigh and so Will and I swapped with her and Mrs Temple.

"What did you wish for, Emma?" she asked. "I wished for a Pop Princess microphone."

"Nina! You can't ask Emma that. You're not supposed to tell people your wishes." Mrs Temple raised her eyebrows at me.

And I was grateful to her, because as I had stood by the well, holding my coin, I realized that as far as wishes went, I was very confused about what I wanted.

The next morning I said I felt ill and wasn't going to ski school. I knew I was being ridiculous, but I just couldn't bear to face Franz in front of everyone. I had made such a big deal of wanting to go out with him and no doubt bored poor Georgia to death droning on about it. And now I felt I'd be letting her down in some way if I told her the truth and that I was having second thoughts.

Georgia was devastated on my behalf.

"Emma, poor you. You must be desperate to see Franz again. Shall I tell him to come and see you later?"

"No! Honestly. Thanks, but I'd rather wait to see him when I'm feeling better."

"Of course. OK, well, we'll see you later." Everyone tramped out, leaving Dad and me at the breakfast table. "Do you want to play cards, Dad?" I asked.

Josie appeared from the kitchen looking stern.

"Your dad needs a walk. He needs daily exercise on those crutches. And *you're* not supposed to be well. Why don't you go and lie down. I'll keep him company." She beamed at him.

I was going to protest, but I wasn't feeling up to a fight with Josie.

I went up to my room and took out my diary as I listened to the front door closing. A while later I heard it open and someone coming up the stairs. There was a knock on the door and Mrs Temple popped her head in.

"Feeling any better?"

I nodded.

"Why don't we go Christmas shopping?" she suggested. "Nina's in ski school and her dad's collecting her today. We could catch the bus to the next town. If you're like me you've still got loads to do."

I smiled gratefully – that sounded perfect, and hopefully it would stop me thinking about the awful situation with Franz. I pulled on some jeans and my grey sweater, and ran downstairs to grab my coat.

"So how are things?" Mrs Temple asked, as we sat in the steamy warmth of the bus.

"Great," I replied.

She nodded. "That's good. I'm delighted that you're all getting on so well."

I smiled enthusiastically. "Georgia's brilliant. I couldn't have wished for anyone nicer to be on holiday with."

"She tells me this Franz of yours is pretty special…"

"Mmm. He is, erm, really nice."

"But she doesn't seem to have met anyone herself yet?"

"Not yet, but *loads* of boys are interested in her!" I checked myself. I didn't want to say too much about Georgia's social life to her mum.

Mrs Temple was looking at me, smiling. "You know it's not always easy to tell if things are going to work out with a boy. If I remember back to my dim and distant youth, there was a lot of trial and error involved."

"Really?" It was hard to imagine Mrs Temple ever going out with anyone except Mr Temple.

"Absolutely. I was always making the wrong

143

choices, thinking I might like this one and that one, and then, out of the blue, the right one came along, and everything just clicked."

"Did it?" I frowned. "Do you think that, perhaps, if you didn't click straight away, if you kept on seeing each other and tried *really* hard, you might click later on?"

"Mmmm." She frowned. "I'm not sure dating should be such hard work!"

I leaned back in my seat. She was right, I knew she was … but I just didn't want to believe it.

The big department stores in the shopping street were strung with twinkling fairy lights, and the windows were decorated with large Christmas scenes. I bought all my presents in one shop – a small leather-bound notebook for Dad, a new ski hat for Will, some marzipan chocolates for Mr and Mrs Temple and something sparkly for Nina and Georgia. I bought Josie some bubble bath that was on special offer.

"What about Adam?" Mrs Temple asked, as I reeled off all my purchases.

"I got his in the village the other day," I replied.

"Well, that's great. You're done. And I've done

everyone, too, even Josie." Mrs Temple beamed as we staggered into the cosy heat of the bus carrying our bags. "She looks after us all so well, doesn't she?"

"I suppose."

Mrs Temple turned to face me. "She's certainly taken care of your father since his accident. To fall and break your ankle on the first day is such a terrible shame. I do feel sorry for him. Thank goodness she's been there to make it a bit easier. He's been on his own for some time, hasn't he?"

"He's got Will and me!"

Mrs Temple looked surprised. "Of course he has! I didn't mean that you don't look out for your dad. Not for one moment; it's obvious that you're all very close... It's just that one day, you know ... he may meet someone..."

"That won't be for ages and ages. He's not ready, not ready at all!" I snapped.

Mrs Temple looked surprised, but said no more on the subject. But the conversation had disturbed me. When we got back I sat in one of the big armchairs in front of the fire brooding to myself. Dad was sat in the other one. He asked about the shopping trip and then he got out his writing pad and I fetched my diary and began to write. Nina and Mr Temple arrived back and immediately grabbed their swimming things and dragged Mrs Temple out for a relaxing soak in the hot tub. As soon as they had gone, Dad seemed to get the hint that I wanted to be left alone and hobbled upstairs for a nap, leaving me to scribble away in peace. I was just getting to the end of my account of the painful events of last night when the others crashed in.

"Well, you weren't missed!" said Will cheerfully, as he collapsed on to the sofa and stretched out his toes towards the fire.

Adam flopped into the chair next to mine, clutching his guitar. He caught sight of my diary. "Don't tell me," he said, "let me guess: 'Dear Diary, met dreamy Austrian boy. I love his *so* much.'" He grinned.

"Don't listen to him!" Georgia cried from the hall. "He's an idiot. And I'm sure Franz missed you loads."

"Question is," Adam asked, looking at me intently and playing a single chord, "did she miss him?"

I looked away.

"He didn't look like he was missing you to me," Will went on before I could think of a reply. "He was chatting away to Georgia all through lunch! And you should thank her for that, Emma – it saved him from Janine's clutches. She was so excited you weren't there today she was practically tap-dancing in front of him on the table. Lucky you've got such a good mate."

Georgia went scarlet.

"Thanks, Georgia," I said dutifully.

"We were talking about the Christmas Party," she explained. "He asked what we were all doing. He's going to juggle. Which reminds me, Will, you said at lunch that you'd help me practise my card trick. I know you only said you'd help me to impress the Irish girl, but I'm holding you to it."

"OK," Will grumbled. "But let's go somewhere where your brilliant technique won't be exposed to curious eyes." They disappeared upstairs, leaving me and Adam alone.

I suddenly felt very self-conscious.

Adam looked up from strumming his guitar, and stared at me again.

"I've been working on this song," he said, fiddling with his guitar strap. I was telling Lenka and Georgia about it earlier. It's a kind of Christmas song."

He played a chord and then slapped his hand on the strings to silence it.

"Is that it?" I joked feebly.

Adam ignored me. "I was hoping to play it at the Christmas Party, the only problem is it hasn't got any lyrics. My mate Chaz usually writes them for our band. So, seeing as you like writing so much, I wondered if you'd be able to help me out. Can I play it to you?"

I nodded.

It was a great tune, sweet and gentle. He played with his head hung low over the guitar. The firelight lit the gold in his hair and the intense expression on his face. I watched him closely as his fingers found the chords, and as I did, the truth I had been trying so hard not to acknowledge suddenly hit me as hard and as fast as the snowy ground the day I fell off the chairlift.

I was completely and totally crazy about Adam Temple.

He looked up at me and grinned. "So what do you think?"

"Yeah, great," I croaked.

"Like I said," he murmured, strumming another chord, "it needs some lyrics. So, can you help me out?"

I opened my mouth, but nothing came out.

He raised an eyebrow at me. "Emma? Are you OK?"

"I'm fine," I said, trying to compose myself. "All right, I'll give it a go," I added, as casually as I could, though my heart was thumping so loudly I was convinced everyone down in the village could hear it.

He gave me a slow smile. "Great, thanks. I loaded the tune on to my iPod before I came out here so you can listen to it as many times as you like. Only if you want to?" He glanced at me anxiously.

"Sure," I replied.

Adam put his hand in his pocket, pulled out his iPod, and handed it over. "Could we try and spend some time on it together tomorrow?"

I looked up at him. Our eyes locked.

"Pick a card! Any card!"

A fan of cards was suddenly thrust in between our two chairs.

Georgia laughed. "This trick is so brilliant, you just *have* to see it…"

"It's Christmas Eve! It's Christmas Eve! Still time for last-minute shopping!" Nina's voice was accompanied by a loud banging on our bedroom door and a slip of paper being slid underneath. Nina had been revising and adding to her present list. Again.

I crawled out of bed, exhausted. Last night, Georgia, tired out from her day on the slopes, had gone to bed early and crashed out straight away. I had stayed awake till about 1am listening to Adam's iPod, and scribbling lyrics on bits of paper until, eventually, I had written a song that worked with his music. I looked at the last lines...

I won't cry when the blue ice melts
And the sleigh bells disappear.
Blow out the candles on the tree
And I won't shed a tear.
When the cold snow goes I won't feel the lows
As the season drifts away...

Cause don't you see, when you smile at me,
Well, I don't feel the weather
'Cause when you gaze into my eyes
It's Christmas Day for ever...

It was painful to think that he'd be thinking about Lenka when he read them. But I just had to face it – they were happy together and I needed to be happy for them, to forget about my stupid feelings and think about theirs. I picked up the lyrics and went downstairs to breakfast.

Lenka smiled up at me from the table.

"Hi, Emma. I thought I'd make an early start and join you for breakfast! Are you feeling better?"

"Yes, thanks," I nodded. "Raring to go!"

"That's good – we missed you yesterday, didn't we, Georgia? And I'm sure Franz did too. You must be happy you're going to see him today – Janine's been trying her best to steal him. Lucky for you Georgia keeps him talking all the time." She leaned into Adam and snatched a bite of his toast.

I watched the two of them as they flirted over their

breakfast, and suddenly I panicked – there was no way I could give Adam the lyrics in front of everyone. What if he read them out and my face gave me away? I was bound to go bright red. I would just have to leave them on the table in his room for him to find later. I stuffed the lyrics into the back pocket of my ski trousers. "Wow! Is that the time?" I grabbed a piece of toast. "Better dash. I want to find my ski legs before the class starts." And I dashed downstairs to get my gear.

I sat on the bench and pulled on my boots. I had to stop thinking about Adam Temple! It was pointless and stupid, stupid, stupid. He had a fantastic girlfriend, who I really liked. I needed to get over this. I had to.

"Looking forward to seeing Gunter again?" Georgia asked, as we clattered into the cable car. I was relieved that it was packed full, and that I could hardly see Will, Lenka and Adam at the other end.

"No!" I wailed. "Take my mind off it by telling me again about how many more perfectly lovely boys you've rejected in the past few days."

She laughed. "It won't be *that* bad, Emma."

But she was wrong. Two pain-free days made it all the harder. Granted I could now snow plough in a wobbly line without falling over every time, but it was hardly enjoyable. My bruises had turned all the colours of the rainbow in the past few days, and now I would be getting some new ones. Apart from Janine, everyone else in our class appeared to be progressing brilliantly. I got out of the cable car and began to put on my skis, blinking in the bright sunlight. I looked around; even though I had a morning of pain ahead of me, I couldn't deny that being up on the mountain was beautiful. I took a deep breath of chilled, fresh air and gently pushed off towards my class. It was good to see their familiar, friendly faces again – apart from Janine's.

I decided to concentrate very hard on my skiing, but it was difficult with so much going on in my head. As I hit the ground for the second time, I wondered if maybe I was imagining my feelings for Adam. After all, I *had* thought I was mad about Franz. As I mulled this over, I became more and more convinced. I'd only been on one date with Franz and I'd completely written it off as another disaster. Maybe we just needed more time. Perhaps Adam and Lenka coming along the path that night had put me off the kiss… What if I kissed Franz again? And made more of an effort this time?

I watched Lenka ski neatly and swiftly past me.

That had to be it. Maybe if I really made a big effort when I saw Franz today, the stupid crush on Adam would go away. I knew I was lucky to be going out with Franz. *All* the girls wanted to go out with him. And what was so special about Adam? His tawny hair was always a mess, he was teasing and sarcastic, he left his sweaters lying around all over the chalet and he stole the pepperoni off your pizza when he thought you weren't looking. You see? Nothing special. I took a deep breath. It was the Christmas Party tonight and I was going to do my best to enjoy it. I was going to shove my hopeless feelings for Adam out of the way and *force* things to work with Franz.

"Emma! You're dreaming again!" Gunter snapped. "Always a dreamer. Concentrate, please." I got up, gritted my teeth and pushed off again down the slope where the others were waiting.

By the end of the lesson, every muscle in my body ached so, in spite of my nerves at seeing Franz again, I couldn't wait to get to the restaurant.

"Hello, Emma." Franz smiled anxiously as he sat down next to me at lunch. I pushed my sunglasses on top of my head and smiled.

"Hello." We looked at each other awkwardly. I wished Georgia was nearer, but she had placed herself as far away as she could, on the other side of the table, and had ignored my desperate eye signals to sit near me. Janine, on the other hand, had made sure that she was sitting on the other side of Franz.

I could feel Franz trying to think of something to say to me at the same time as I tried to think of something to say to *him*.

"How's the slalom going?" I asked at the same time as he said, "I hope you feel better today."

I gave a nervous laugh and gestured for him to speak first.

"Slalom is going well," he replied.

"Great," I smiled encouragingly. "My skiing isn't getting any better. Janine and I don't seem to be getting anywhere."

"Like it's my fault!" Janine snorted. "It's that ancient

155

gnome of a ski instructor. He has no *idea* how to teach properly…"

She ran her fingers through her hair and gazed at Franz. "What *I* really need is some extra lessons…"

Franz turned to me.

"Can we talk, just us, after lunch?"

"Sure," I said quickly. If it meant we didn't have to have a conversation now, with everyone listening to every word, then that was fine by me. We both relaxed and joined in the general conversation around the table. There was more talk about the party and a heated discussion about which act was going to be the best.

After we'd finished eating, I caught Franz's eye and we got up.

"Where are you two going?" Janine asked, irritated.

"Just for a wander," I replied, trying to sound casual. Adam looked up and stared at us momentarily before turning to say something to Lenka. I picked up my gloves and gave Franz a beaming smile. I had to forget about Adam Temple.

Franz took me to a bench under the dining terrace and we sat down. It was rather gloomy under there, but at least it was private. At last a chance to kiss with no one around. Hopefully this time it would be brilliant and everything would be as it should be.

"Emma," Franz said cautiously. "You are a very nice girl, very nice…"

Nice? Was "nice" good? I decided to look at his long blond hair and tanned face and not let myself get distracted by what he was saying.

He coughed. "I want to say something more. I think you are a very pretty girl too…"

OK, I thought, *you think I'm a nice girl and I'm pretty. I think you're a nice boy and you're not bad-looking, either. Can we just get on with this kiss because I'm trying so, so, hard to make this work…*

"I think we both knew something after our date, didn't we?"

I nodded seriously.

He relaxed a bit. "So you understand?"

I nodded again. He smiled at me and leaned forward.

Here we go! I yelled inside. I lunged forward, planting my lips on his.

We remained motionless with our lips pressed

together. *Is this it?* I wondered, keeping my eyes tightly closed. *Because if it is, it's even worse than last time.*

After a few moments I opened my eyes and pulled away. He was looking at me with a shocked expression. A wave of embarrassment flowed over me as I spotted his ski pass on the ground. *That* was what he was leaning towards...

"Oh dear," I murmured. "You weren't expecting that, were you?"

He shook his head.

"We're not really good together in a boyfriend and girlfriend way, are we?" I blurted out. "I expect that was what you were trying to say, wasn't it?"

He nodded.

He was right, of course, and I knew it. I had been an idiot to think forcing myself to like him in that way was going to work. Now *he* knew I was an idiot, too. I looked up at his face. He was as red as I was.

I took a deep breath and sat up straight. "That's OK. We can just be friends."

Somehow I had to cover up my humiliation. This was the second boy who had dumped me after just one date. I had made a complete mess of things again and it was all my fault. I hadn't listened to a word Natalie or Parisa had said. I'd come straight out to Austria and made exactly the same mistake. But I'd learned my lesson, I really had, because I'd found a boy I could talk to about anything, a boy I wanted to spend every minute with and who made me laugh more than any boy I'd ever met. It's just that he'd found a girl he felt the same way about. And it was Lenka.

Franz was still looking troubled.

"What's up? Is there something else you want to say?" I asked.

"I must tell the truth, Emma. You see I think you ought to know, I like someone else."

"Well, that's OK!" I managed to smile, biting back the words, *Me too*.

"Does she like you?" I asked instead. "God, it's not Janine, is it? Because I'm never one to interfere, but really I can't see that working out well for either of you…"

He smiled. "No, it's not Janine."

I relaxed. "Well, who is it then? Do I know her?"

"You know her very well."

I stared at him, and then cried out, "Georgia!"

He nodded. I sat back on the bench.

"Well, I don't know why I'm so surprised – you've got on brilliantly since that day you went to the waterfall." I frowned. "What I don't understand is why you didn't ask her out in the first place…"

He smiled. "Georgia spent the whole afternoon talking about *you* – how funny you are, how clever. I thought she couldn't be interested in me because if she had been, she wouldn't have said all that stuff. It was obvious she wanted me to ask *you* out." He shrugged. "And you *are* a very pretty girl…"

He grinned at me. I grinned back.

"Does she know how you feel?" I asked.

"I don't know. We get on really well, but I think even if she did like me, she wouldn't show it, as she'd be worried that it would spoil your friendship."

"Well, you must make your feelings known straight away. Trust me – the two of you getting together wouldn't bother me at all, in fact I'd be really pleased. I know she thinks you're the best company *and*," I smiled at him, "you *are* a very pretty boy."

He laughed. "Are you sure you don't mind?"

"No, and anyway, it wouldn't be the point if I did.

You like her and she likes you – you're far better suited than we are. I mean, look how much better we're getting on now we can just be friends. And do you know what? I think she's been nuts about you the whole time."

I stood up. "I'll tell her this afternoon that we're no longer going out. We never really were, were we?"

He shook his head. "She is a very lovely person – Georgia."

I smiled. "She really, really is."

I thought about how I had droned on and on about Franz to her. No wonder she hadn't dared tell me her true feelings as she had grown to realize that she liked him herself. It must have been so hard for her, and I never even noticed. I felt like a rubbish friend as well as a rubbish girlfriend.

We strolled back up to the restaurant. "I'll see you tonight, Emma!" he said, as he put on his skis.

"Absolutely! And go for it … she's a lovely girl!" He waved a ski pole at me as he set off in the direction of the village.

Adam was standing alone at the bottom of the restaurant steps. "Is everything OK?"

"Well, we're over, if that's what you mean…"

He looked concerned. "And you're fine about it?"

"Yes, I am. In fact, I'm a bit relieved to be honest."

He reached out and touched my arm. "Look, I need to talk to you…"

I glanced up at him – his grey eyes were even more intense than usual.

"Hey, Emma!" a voice called. "I thought I'd wait for you." Lenka waved, as she and Will appeared at the top of the steps.

"Come on, Adam. What are we waiting for?" Will raced over to fetch his skis. "Let's get going."

Adam tore his gaze away and followed Will over to the rack. "OK. See you later, you two."

Lenka smiled at me. "Georgia's already gone down with the others. They're all going swimming. Are you coming?" she asked, as we collected our skis.

I wondered if Georgia had gone because she didn't want to be around Franz and me.

"Thanks for waiting, Lenka, but I think I might go and keep my dad company at the chalet."

She peered at me. "Are you all right, Emma?"

"It's over with Franz and me; he ended it, but it

never really began," I sighed.

There was only one boy that I wanted to be with, and he was out of bounds. I'd been so caught up in my Austrian dream boy plans, I hadn't realized what had been staring me in the face the whole time.

"Are you sure you're OK?" asked Lenka.

"I'm fine, really – we get on much better as friends."

"Well that's good that you're both happy." I noticed a shadow cross her face.

"Aren't *you* happy?" I asked.

Because if I was going out with Adam Temple, I thought, *I'd be the happiest girl in the whole world.*

She tossed back her hair. "Yes, sure I am. Adam is wonderful. I'm very happy. He's the handsome English boy I told all my friends back home I'd find, and I did, but," she pulled a face, "but... maybe... I'm not so sure he's happy. His mind seems far away. I've never had this with a boy before."

I forced myself to joke. "You should try being me. The only two boys I've been out with both finished with me after one date!"

"That means they weren't the right boys!" she said firmly, then looked serious. "I'd like to do something at the party tonight to make Adam, you know … pay attention. He will play his guitar, but I have nothing I can do – I can't sing or do anything. I just want to impress him … to pull him back… Do you understand?"

I thought about Georgia and what she had done for me, even though she really liked Franz.

That was being a real friend.

Perhaps this was the time to show that I could be one, too.

I forced my hand into the back pocket of my ski trousers and pulled out the crumpled page of lyrics.

"Here," I said, handing it over, and forcing a smile. "I scribbled these for his song last night as he mentioned he needed some lyrics… You take them. Say you wrote them – just write them out again in your own writing."

Her mouth dropped open. "Emma! You are so kind. Are you sure? Don't you want to give them to Adam yourself?"

"No," I lied. I gazed out at the blue sky over the mountains. "They're not important to me. Not important at all…"

When Georgia got back from the pool, it was obvious that Lenka had told her about Franz and me because she followed me around until we got up to our room.

"How are you?" she asked, as soon as we were inside. "Lenka said you were fine about Franz, but I don't see how *that* can be true. And if it means so little to you, why do you look so sad? Please don't let it spoil the party for you."

"Are *you* looking forward to the party?"

She blushed.

"I didn't tell Lenka the whole story about Franz." I brushed my hair back. "There was something else."

"What?"

"He's crazy about someone..."

Georgia gazed at me. "Really? Do you know who?"

"Yes, it's some English girl he finds completely and utterly fascinating – a slim, fair-haired girl, who's a pretty good skier now and a bit bonkers about rocks..."

A scarlet flush sped up Georgia's face. "Emma, I never, *ever—*"

"And she's also the most loyal, trustworthy and kind friend a girl could ever hope to have," I interrupted, and went over to give her a big hug.

I drew back. "I'm so, so sorry. I've been the worst friend ever. All I've done is go on and on about my Austrian dream boy like it was the most important thing in the world, and I've totally ignored your feelings. I feel such an idiot. I couldn't have been more wrong about everything. It's you Franz is crazy about."

She gave me a serious look. "I … I … don't know what to say; I mean I do really like him. But *honestly* only if you truly don't mind."

"Of course I don't. You two have got so much in common. I'm only grateful Franz had the courage to say something. We were never right for each other."

Georgia leaped up. "I've got to get ready for the party! Oh my God. I've got nothing to wear."

I laughed at her nerves. "Don't panic. We've got hours! I'll help you." I went out on to the landing and banged on the shower door. "Get out of there, Will! Here come the girls!"

An hour and a half later, and with the contents of our wardrobe in a heap on the floor, we were almost ready. Our preparations had not been without interruptions. Dad, and Mr and Mrs Temple kept popping in asking to borrow strange things like beads and blusher and black eye-liner. We had showered and done our hair. I had put Georgia's up in a diamante clip and she had blow-dried mine shiny and straight. After trying on about a hundred different outfits, Georgia settled on my black silky top, which she wore with her black mini. She looked down at her legs. "These thick black tights are awful. I wish I had something a bit more elegant."

I rummaged around in my top drawer and handed her a small package. "Here, early Christmas present." She unwrapped a pair of sparkly tights and hugged me. "Thank you so much! They're perfect."

Nina popped her head round the door. "Can I have my present now too?"

"No! You'll be sad tomorrow morning if you do," I laughed.

"I won't. I promise."

I looked at Nina all dressed up in her shimmering pale blue party dress, her hair tied back in a blue ribbon.

"Actually, it would sort of go with what you're wearing... Oh, go on then." I fished out a small parcel and handed it to Nina. She tore off the wrapper in seconds.

"A bracelet! It's lovely. It even matches my dress! Thank you." Nina put it on and admired her wrist.

"Now off you go and leave us to finish getting dressed." Georgia shooed her out.

"You'd better hurry," Nina called over her shoulder. "The boys were ready ages ago – everyone's waiting downstairs."

Georgia and I had a last look in the mirror and checked each other's make-up. Lipgloss, mascara, eyeliner – all good. I pushed my feet into my white ballet pumps. They matched my white silky mini dress with the gold ribbon that tied in the front perfectly.

"Are you sure I look OK?" Georgia asked me, nervously fiddling with her necklace.

I stopped at the door and looked at her. "Georgia, you look absolutely beautiful. He's going to think he's the luckiest boy in the world."

"I hope so," she sighed.

When we got downstairs Will was at the card table having a ferocious game of Snap with Dad and Mr Temple. Mr Temple was wearing flared trousers, a waistcoat and a painted-on moustache. Dad was dressed in a magician's outfit – bow tie, tails and top hat. Goodness knows where he'd got it from. I allowed myself a quick glance at Adam – he was sitting in one of the armchairs strumming his guitar. He was wearing a pair of black denim jeans and his grey shirt. His newly washed hair shone and his grey eyes stood out even more now his face was so tanned. Sitting there with his guitar he looked like a rock star.

"Well! Look at you two," Dad cried. "You both look lovely."

"Absolutely stunning, both of you," agreed Mr Temple. Georgia beamed and went over to join them. "Now we're just waiting for my gorgeous Cher."

"I'm right here, Sonny," said Mrs Temple, appearing from the kitchen with a glass of wine. She was wearing a long black wig, headband and hippie beads.

I sat down on the other armchair, took my diary out of my bag and pretended to be writing.

A minute later, Nina's nose thrust itself between me and the pages. "Do you always write upside down?" She chattered on, not waiting for an answer. "I've just asked Georgia about your boyfriend, and she says he's not your boyfriend any more. Is that true?"

"That's right, Nina, he's not."

"Do you think it's because Adam didn't give you good advice on your practice date? You should have asked *me*, not him. He doesn't know *anything*."

Adam put down his guitar and twisted himself round in his chair to look at me. "Nina, go away, I need to speak to Emma."

Nina glared at her brother. "I'm allowed to *talk* ... and I haven't shown her my gold shoes." She lifted a foot and dangled it in front of me.

"Go away, Nina ... *please*." She glared at him, but when she saw his face she put her gold foot down and danced over to join the card table.

I looked up at Adam, my heart beating wildly. His serious face and intense stare were really unnerving.

"What's with the face?" I said, trying to lighten the moment. "You look like you've got something really bad to tell me."

For the first time since I'd met him, Adam looked uncomfortable. "Sorry things didn't work out with Franz," he mumbled. "I wanted to talk to you after lunch, but there was no time. Are you OK?"

"I'm fine, honestly; it really wasn't right from the beginning. But thanks for asking."

"Mmm. I know what you mean," he mused. "Some things aren't meant to be."

"No, they aren't," I agreed, thinking, *If only you knew how true that was.* "So," I said, desperate to change the subject, "how's the music going?" and then I regretted that immediately.

"Great. I wondered if you'd had any time to write anything. I didn't like to ask, but if you have, it'd be good to find a quiet space somewhere where I could practise the lyrics and you could talk me through them."

I looked back down at my diary.

"I'm really sorry, but I didn't get a chance."

A flash of disappointment crossed his face and then he nodded. "Oh, OK, well, it doesn't matter … I can play one of my other songs."

The doorbell rang and Adam leaped up to get it.

Moments later, Dizzy, Bella, Hamish, Ian, Gordon

and Lenka crashed into the sitting room. They were all dressed up for their acts.

Adam sidled up to Lenka and tried to say something to her, but she smiled distractedly and pointed at Dad, who was now standing in the middle of the room with a pencil and paper in his hand.

"So, what is everyone doing? Are we all ready to rehearse?" he shouted. I watched him take control of the proceedings. In spite of his costume he did look very handsome. I could see from the glances that Josie was giving him that she thought so too. Maybe Will and I were just thinking of ourselves, but every time I thought about Josie living in our house and telling us what to do, I felt my blood run cold. She was so totally wrong for Dad, so neat and controlling. She was acting as his assistant tonight and had stunned us all by coming down in a very low-cut waistcoat, hot pants and fishnets. Mrs Temple had choked on her glass of Chardonnay when she saw her and nearly swallowed a lock of her long black wig.

Dizzy and Bella were in ill-fitting men's suits, which they had borrowed from their dads; their hair was tied back and they had fake stubble drawn on their jawlines.

Hamish and Ian were also in suits. "We've come as Take That," Dizzy cried. "We're going to mime though."

They all stood in a row and began to sing very badly, doing all the actions.

"Just as well you are miming," Nina piped up.

Gordon was playing a piece on the piano, so obviously he couldn't rehearse in the chalet, but Georgia tried out her magic trick on everyone and it worked a treat. Dizzy told us that Janine was going to sing "Crazy in Love", by Beyonce. Apparently, she had a singing and drama coach in America and had spent the entire afternoon resting her vocal chords.

"So what are you two doing, Will and Emma?" Dad asked, looking at us.

"My new Spanish girlfriend is big on flamenco dancing and I'm going to accompany her," Will said proudly. "I'm meeting her at the hotel."

"New Spanish girlfriend?" I repeated. "Since when? I thought your latest love interest was Irish."

"Not any more." Will grinned. "Keep up, Emma!"

"Well, what are you accompanying her on?" I asked grumpily. "You can't play anything."

Will bowed his head. "I will be accompanying her

with my," he flourished his hands before us, "clapping."

"*Clapping? That's* your talent?" I snorted.

"Well, what's your contribution, Miss Snooty?"

The room went quiet and everyone looked at me.

"Erm, nothing. I couldn't think of anything."

"Honestly, Emma, you might have at least *tried*," Will said sanctimoniously. He did a few smug claps and *Olè*'s around the room.

Dad frowned. "That's unlike you, Emma, especially when everyone else has made such an effort."

I shrugged and looked away. If only he knew how long I'd worked on those lyrics.

"OK," Dad continued, "well that leaves Adam, who's playing his guitar … and what about you, Lenka? Or will you be joining Emma on the subs bench?"

Lenka beamed. "I have done something for Adam."

Adam turned to look at her in surprise.

"I know Adam is playing a new song, but I heard he had no lyrics for it, so I've written some words."

Adam looked over at her, confused.

She opened her bag and took out a piece of paper. "I hope these are OK, Adam. You still have time to practise if you like them!"

"Well, thanks, Lenka," Adam said. "That's great. That really is so kind of you … I had no idea."

"It's nothing," she smiled. "No problem."

He scanned the words. "But this must have taken you ages." He looked up into her face. She raised her eyebrows and shrugged. "It was fun. I thought you'd like it."

"Aaaaah. Isn't that the sweetest thing?" Dizzy cooed. Adam gave a tense smile and then disappeared to rehearse in his room.

I felt tears begin to prick my eyes and so I was very grateful when Mrs Temple cried out, "Nina's turn now!"

Nina stood up on the sofa and I gave her the thumbs up.

Mr Temple turned on the CD player. Nina took a deep breath and began to sing "Somewhere Over the Rainbow" in her clear, pure voice. When she had finished, all the girls were sniffling and dabbing away their tears, so no one noticed mine.

Georgia and I held on to each other's arms as we walked carefully along the icy path to the waiting taxi. Most of our party was going to walk through the woods, but girls in party shoes were being taken by car.

"Are you excited?" I asked her.

"Like you can't imagine," she whispered. "I can't believe this is really happening to me! But what about *you*? Are you all right?"

"I'm fine!" I lied.

"You would tell me if there was anything wrong? You seemed a bit quiet earlier."

"I'm absolutely great, honestly," I beamed.

Nina skipped up beside me. "Can I sit with you at the party tonight?" she asked.

"Sure," I smiled, pulling my scarf tighter round my neck against the cold night air.

"Good, we can be like judges on the telly." She watched her breath come out like smoke. "You can be

176

the kind one and I'll be the horrible one who tells the truth. Aren't you so excited that it's nearly Christmas?"

I smiled at her. "I can't wait," I said.

Five minutes later, our taxi was pulling up in front of the hotel. It was big and old-fashioned, its facade strung with twinkling lights. Four fir trees in gold pots lined the wide stone steps leading up to it. Inside, huge antlers draped with tinsel were mounted on the walls. The banisters were decorated with garlands of pine branches and gold and green ribbons. We handed in our coats and headed for the function room.

A large chandelier lit with real candles hung from the ceiling and a tall tree, decorated in white and gold glass baubles, towered in the corner. A small stage had been errected at the far end. Everyone was dressed up. I looked down at my little white dress to make sure that the gold ribbon was tied properly at the front.

"You can feel it's Christmas, can't you?" Nina gasped excitedly, doing a little skip in her gold shoes.

Mrs Temple swooped down to scoop up a glass of champagne from a passing tray. "I'm going to need a few of these before I do my Cher impression in front of all these people," she laughed.

Janine appeared in a tight red sequinned dress, her eyes scanning the room. She was clearly looking for someone … and I had a hunch who it was.

I couldn't help smiling as, moments later, Franz walked straight past her towards a blushing Georgia.

"What is it with those English girls!" Janine shouted so we could all hear. "What's so special about *them!*"

The entertainment began and everyone did their turn. There was the horrendous shock of seeing Gunter's gnarled little legs in a pair of *lederhosen* doing an Austrian dance. Then, after a feast of yodelling, opera singing and folk musicians, it was Dad's turn to perform his magic tricks.

Nina leaned into me. "I'm afraid Josie's trying to be too sexy, aren't you?" she observed primly.

"Nina!" I exclaimed, but I did have to agree. I was glad she was there with her mad commentary – it was just the distraction I needed. When it was her go and she hopped on to the stage and sang her song, note perfect, no one clapped or cheered harder than me. She sat back down again, beaming with pride.

"Full marks, best singer of the night by a mile. Has a brilliant future ahead of her…" I cried.

Next up was Will.

The Spanish girl came on with a shawl draped round her hips, and began to stamp her feet in time to the music. Then she was off, moving around the stage with electrifying energy. She was brilliant.

"Pity Will is totally out of time?" Nina whispered. "But I'm giving him a high mark for looking like he's really enjoying himself and for, erm … enthusiasm."

We judged away until there were only two acts left. Janine and Adam. I had avoided being anywhere near Adam all evening, but by the look of it, so had Lenka. After we arrived I had lost track of her and now she was sitting on the other side of the room, deep in conversation with Georgia and Franz.

Janine stepped up on to the stage. I could see her mother in a feathered halter neck watching her every move. We all stared at the stage in anticipation.

She took the microphone off the stand. "Tonight, ladies and gentlemen, I shall be singing 'Crazy in Love' by Beyonce."

Her mum turned on the CD player and she was off.

Three minutes later there was a smattering of polite applause from around the shell-shocked room.

Nina stared at me, open-mouthed.

"That was the worst singing I have ever heard," she gasped. "Even worse than Mum's."

But I wasn't listening because Adam was walking on to the stage holding his guitar and suddenly I couldn't see or hear anything else in the room.

He dragged up a chair and sat down, adjusting the mike. He checked the tuning on his guitar and then looked up, his eyes taking in the crowd. "Well, good evening, everyone. I wrote the music for the song I'm going to sing, but it's the words that are the important thing, and I'd like to thank the girl who wrote them, because, well ... I haven't known her long and she's made my holiday so much fun. So I want to say thank you to her by trying to sing these words like they really mean something to me, which they do."

His head dropped down over his guitar and he began to sing.

"Wow!" Nina hissed in my ear. "I've never known Adam say anything like that before about a girl. He must *really* like Lenka."

As I listened to my words fill the room I looked across to see what Lenka was making of it, but in the dimmed lights I couldn't see her expression. It felt so brilliant to hear Adam singing my words, but so painful to know he wasn't thinking of me as he sang them.

When he had finished there was a huge round of applause. Dizzy, Bella, Will and the Spanish girl, Franz and Georgia went up to the stage to congratulate him. I hung back. I didn't need to witness Lenka's reaction to what he'd just said about her. It was a relief when I spotted Mrs Temple coming over to collect a reluctant Nina. I looked around the room – everyone was having a brilliant time … everyone except me, and I wasn't going to let my misery spoil it for them.

"I think I'll come back with you," I said quickly.

Mrs Temple looked surprised. "Really? Don't you want to stay? The disco's about to start and your dad and the others will be here for a while yet."

"No, thanks. I'd rather go back."

She looked at my face and put her arm round me. "That's fine, Emma. You walk back with us then. But your shoes … we've brought a change with us."

"I'll be fine. I'll just go and get my coat."

I walked out of the hot, crowded room and I didn't look back.

18

"Hey, Bambi. Where d'you think you're going?"

I was at the bottom of the hotel steps with Mrs Temple and Nina, wondering how on earth I was going to make it home through all that snow in my ballet pumps. We all stopped and looked back to where Adam was standing outside the entrance.

"I'm still not feeling great," I murmured, "so I'm going to go back with your mum and Nina."

"Wait for me," he said. "I'll get my coat."

Mrs Temple looked at me. "Well, it's started to snow again so I think we'll be getting along. See you back at the chalet, Emma." She propelled a protesting Nina along the pavement before I could say a word.

"So what's all this about?" Adam asked, as he reappeared, pulling his scarf round his neck and staring straight into my eyes in that disconcerting Temple way. "Was it my singing? I know I didn't have that much time to rehearse, but I *could* take offence."

I smiled. "It wasn't your singing; you were ... brilliant, actually."

"So you liked it?"

I nodded.

"Like the lyrics?"

I dodged a group of people laughing and celebrating on the pavement and skidded on my slippery shoes. Adam grabbed my arm and steadied me.

"Because I thought they were fantastic." He let go of me. "And I meant what I said, you know ... about the person who wrote them."

I managed a tight smile. "Well, that's good. She is a lovely girl. And she really likes you too."

"Really?" He smiled. "I'm glad to hear that. Very glad."

I skidded again and this time he held on to my arm and steered me through the crowded street.

"So why don't you go back to the hotel, then?" I couldn't help asking.

The sound of fireworks crackled around us and lit up the sky. In the village square a brass band was playing "Silent Night". I wasn't sure he had heard the question at all, as the next thing he said was, "Do you want to walk back along the lake? The moon is really bright tonight, so we could cut through the woods afterwards. We'll easily be able to see our way."

I stopped and looked down at my shoes; walking through the woods was not going to be easy, moon or no moon.

"Won't the others be wondering where you are?"

"Maybe, but Mum and Nina are way ahead now and I can't let you go back on your own. I'm committed to your safe delivery."

I felt confused. Surely escorting me home was the last thing he wanted to do, when he could have been dancing the night away with Lenka. And although it was lovely to have his company, it just made me feel worse inside.

"I'll be fine. Honestly. You go back to the hotel. You don't have to walk with me."

"Ah, but I do. I know you well enough by now to realize that you can barely walk two steps without falling over."

"So untrue!" I began to stride ahead, desperately trying to keep my balance. He raced past me, turned round and began walking backwards.

"Nina says it was me that trashed your date with Franz. She says I failed to give you even half-decent advice."

I smiled. "It wasn't anything to do with your advice. Franz is great – we just didn't 'click', that's all."

"Didn't click?"

I took a deep breath. "You know … neither of us felt that spark that you feel when…"

"When it's really working?"

"Yes." We were nearing the outskirts of the village now and Adam walked alongside me as we turned down the path that led towards the lake.

"Remember when we went skating?" he said, as we came out from the trees. The pale white expanse of frozen water looked ghostly in the moonlight. I pulled my coat tighter round me.

"You did the skating and I did the falling over, if I remember rightly. And anyway, we didn't skate here," I said simply.

"I know. But we had a good time on that local rink, didn't we?"

"You said I was like a sack of potatoes!" I protested, but I couldn't help smiling at the memory.

185

"You said I was whiney."

"You were. But you obviously listened to my advice on your real date," I couldn't resist saying. "So I'm glad I was of assistance."

A flurry of snow danced around us as Adam pushed a branch out of our way.

"Oh, you were helpful." He was walking very close to me now. I could see the snowflakes nestled in his hair. "I thought about what you said the whole evening. But I think you need to add something else about me to your list."

"What's that?"

"Seriously stupid."

I looked up sharply. "I don't think that."

Adam shook his head. "Oh, but you do. In fact I think you think I'm the stupidest boy you've ever met."

"I don't think you're stupid," I protested. "Lots of other things, yes, but not stupid."

He stopped walking and pulled me to a halt.

"So why on earth did you imagine for one minute that I would think Lenka had written those lyrics?"

My heart started thumping. He knew. Was this what it was all about? He had worked out that I was crazy about him, and had come to tell me … what? *I'm sorry, Emma, I know you like me, but you have to understand I'm with someone else…?*

I blushed, pulled away and carried on walking. "She did. She really did."

He hurried after me. "OK, I'm now writing down 'Massive Liar' on my list. I know you wrote them, Emma; no one else could have, least of all Lenka. I was stunned when she produced them, and then when I sat down and read them properly I knew for sure that they were yours. And besides, Lenka didn't have my iPod, so how could she even have known the tune? Explain that."

"I sang it to her," I said desperately.

Adam burst out laughing. "Oh, really? Is that right? You sang it to her? That would be during ski class, would it? And then she wrote the lyrics, just like that."

"Yes. And I'm writing 'Disbelieving' and 'Sarcastic' now," I cried, slipping and sliding along the icy path.

"You've already got 'Sarcastic', you can't have it twice."

"I can. I can have whatever I like on my list."

The snow was falling thicker and faster as we

reached the path that led into the woods. "Why don't you go back to the hotel – Lenka will be wondering where you've got to. I really will be fine from here," I said. I began to walk quickly up through the trees, but I could hear him following me. I broke into a trot, trying to dodge the rocks and branches in the moonlight, willing him to disappear. I didn't want to have this conversation. If I admitted I'd written the lyrics, it wouldn't take a genius to work out what I really felt ... and how embarrassing would that be? I took my eye off the path for a moment to look for the light of the chalet through the trees and my foot hit a root. The next moment, someone crashed into me, sending me flying, and I landed flat on my face in the snow.

"You see?" said a voice in my ear. "This is *exactly* what I was talking about. You are simply not capable of walking upright like the rest of us and now I expect it's going to be the 'sack of potatoes' scenario all over again."

"Go away," I muttered, brushing some snow off my face. "I'm perfectly fine on my own, thank you very much."

"Well, that's a relief, as I think I've done myself a

serious injury." He rolled over on to his back, clutching at his leg. "But don't worry about me – off you go. When you come back in the morning, just look for a big white mound and start digging."

I raised myself painfully on to my elbows to look at him. He stared back, and my heart gave a jolt. "Have you really hurt yourself?"

He grabbed my arm and pulled me gently towards him. "No, I haven't. Look, Emma," he said seriously, "I'm not kidding around now. And if you'd just be quiet for two minutes, I'll explain. Lenka and I are over. I was going to finish it at the chalet before the party, but then you pulled the lyrics stunt and I got caught by surprise and felt embarrassed because for one really mad moment I thought she *had* written them. And don't try and deny it again. But what I don't understand is, why on earth did you *do* that?"

My mind was in a whirl trying to process what he had said, so I blurted out the first thought that came into my head, which happened to be the truth. "Because she really liked you and she wanted to impress you. I wanted to be a good friend and help her out."

"Emma, no lyrics in the world were going to make

things work out between Lenka and me. We just didn't have that spark that you were talking about."

"But she's gorgeous and kind and interesting. How could you not think she's great?" I cried.

"I do think she's great. Like you think Franz is great, but who knows what makes things work between people. Nothing worked with her like it did when we went out together."

I felt my heartbeat quicken. "So if you felt this way about Lenka from the start, why did you carry on?"

"Same reason that you kept persevering with Franz, I expect," said Adam. "I hoped things would get better … but they didn't. And by then I'd realized I was with the wrong girl, but you were so full of your date with Franz that I didn't think I stood a chance. And then when you ducked out of ski school the morning after your date, I felt more hopeful that you might not be having such a good time after all, which is why I asked you to write the lyrics. I knew you'd be brilliant at it and I hoped it would give me an excuse to spend a bit of time with you."

I stared into his face, trying to take in what he was saying. Adam Temple was crazy about me!

He brushed some snow from my hair. "We did have a good time, didn't we? On our practice date?" His hand was running through my hair now. It felt electric.

"We did," I managed to say. He pulled me closer. "I seem to remember that there was one category that we didn't test, and I feel in the interest of our research that we shouldn't leave it out."

"And what category would that be?" I smiled.

"This one," he murmured, and kissed me.

A while later I drew back and looked into his face.

The kiss had been everything I had imagined a kiss should be. Natalie could write "dreamy" and "thrilling" in her notebook and underline it a hundred times now.

"So what's my score?" I asked, smiling.

"Hmm ... now let me see – is this category marked out of ten?"

I nodded.

"Well, in that case I'll have to do a re-test, just to double check I've got your score correct."

He gently pulled me towards him again, whispering, "Which was ten out of ten, by the way."

"Get up, get up! It's Christmas Day!"

I heard Mr Temple groan from his room. "It's five o'clock in the morning, Nina!"

"But I've been downstairs and Father Christmas has been and the presents are all there. I've already opened my stocking. I can't wait any longer. *Please...*"

Which is how we all found ourselves a short while later, bleary-eyed in our dressing gowns, drinking hot chocolate and opening presents. Only Josie was still in bed.

Adam caught my eye as he came into the sitting room, and I couldn't help smiling from ear to ear. This had to be the best Christmas morning ever.

I thought back to last night. We had arrived home, soaked and freezing, but giggling like lunatics. Mrs Temple had taken in the new development in one single gaze. She'd tutted at the state of us, but I could see she was smiling as she shooed me upstairs to have a hot shower and directed Adam to her bathroom. Ten minutes later, I'd come back downstairs feeling toasty warm in Adam's black sweater. Mrs Temple had appeared from the kitchen with a plate of toasted sandwiches and joined us in a hotly-contended game of Snap in front of the fire.

When the others eventually arrived home she'd sent all of us straight to bed. "You'll all be up early in the morning. Time to get some sleep!" Adam had caught my eye as Georgia and I said our goodnights to them all. I didn't think I would be able to sleep a wink. I had too much to think about. I could tell immediately that Georgia had also had a brilliant evening.

"Was it amazing?" I'd whispered, as we climbed into our beds.

"So amazing!" she'd sighed before checking herself. "Sorry, Emma, that was a bit insensitive."

I'd turned to face her. "Look, Georgia, there's something I need to tell you."

"What? Oh my God—" She pulled her duvet over her head. "You haven't decided you like Franz after all, have you?"

"No, of course not. But there is someone else I like."

She pulled her duvet down again.

"Really! That's brilliant. Oh, by the way, guess what? Adam and Lenka are over."

"I know," I said quietly.

"She was a bit upset at first, but then she told me that she always knew it wasn't really working out. It was just that she'd never had a boy not be crazy about her before, so it was more of a pride thing. And she said if she was honest she found him a bit rude and sarcastic. Well, that's Adam for you. He'll be lucky if he finds a girl with the same sense of humour as him. No one's going to find that part of his personality attractive."

"I do," I said simply.

"And then Lenka got chatted up by Spanish girl's fit brother and perked up no end ... snogging their heads off by the end— *What did you say?*"

Georgia had stared at me, wide-eyed.

"I said I find Adam attractive, even his sarcastic sense of humour; erm ... we kind of got it together this evening on the way home from the party. It's a long story, but it *was* over between Adam and Lenka before anything happened between us, I promise. I hope you don't mind."

She flopped back and stared at the ceiling. "*Mind*! Of course I don't mind, if that's really what you want, but I have to say that I fear for your sanity." She turned back to me again. "*Adam*? Are you crazy?"

"He's gorgeous, Georgia…"

She put her fingers in her ears and began to sing. "La la la la… I think I can just about cope with this, Emma – as long as you don't say words like 'gorgeous' in the same sentence as 'Adam', OK?"

"OK." I laughed.

She began to giggle. "I really can't believe it. It's too weird. What took you so long then? No, don't answer that… What a night!"

"You two," Mr Temple had called out from the landing, "stop your chattering, it's time for bed; the sooner you get to sleep the sooner it'll be morning."

"I can't believe you both gave each other notebooks," Will sighed. He was sitting on the floor in a pile of wrapping paper. "How boring is that?"

"But they're for different things," I explained. "Adam's is for writing music in…"

195

"And Emma's is for writing writing in … I couldn't help noticing that diary you've been scribbling in is nearing the end of its days." Adam grinned at me. We were facing each other, leaning against the armrests at opposite ends of the sofa with our feet up in front of us, nearly touching in the middle.

"I can't believe we went to the same shop in the village and bought practically the same thing for each other." I smiled.

"Oh God," Will groaned. "I don't think I can take any more of you two being nice to each other."

Adam had broken the news to Will last night and he was still in shock.

"Why so grumpy, Will, or should I say Mr *Olè*?!" I asked. "Miss Spain not working out?"

Will closed his eyes. "I'm not seeing Consuela any more – if that's who you're talking about."

"Why not?" Georgia asked, scrabbling to find an earring that Franz had given her that she'd dropped into the pile of wrapping paper.

"She said my clapping wasn't up to standard."

"So not true, bro!" I shouted loyally. "You had … what did you say Will had, Nina?" I called.

Nina turned, holding her wobbly Pop Princess tiara in place. "Enthusiasm," she called back. Her attention was now caught by Adam and me. She stared hard for a moment. "Is Adam your boyfriend now, Emma? Because I can see your toes touching on the sofa."

"Shhhh," I said, going red and quickly moving my feet back. I could see Dad exchange a grin with Mr and Mrs Temple as they disappeared into the kitchen in search of some champagne.

"Yes, they are boyfriend and girlfriend, Nina. But the really exciting news is that they're getting married!" Will said, giving me his "revenge is sweet" smile. I threw a ball of wrapping paper at him.

"Really?" Nina asked, wide-eyed.

"*And* Georgia's going to marry Franz," Will went on.

"Stop it, Will." Georgia laughed. "No one's getting married, Nina." Nina looked at her, disappointed. "*Really*," Georgia said firmly. "No one." She looked across at Will. "And don't take it out on us just because your girlfriend didn't work out."

"All that effort and I wasn't appreciated," Will went on. "But to be honest we didn't have a lot in common."

"There you go, Will," I leaped in. "If you *will* go for looks alone, it's never a guarantee that you're going to get on, you know."

Will threw back his head and guffawed. "What! That's rich coming from you, Emma! You're not telling me that you liked Sam Harrison and Franz because of all the wonderful things you had in common, are you?"

"I've learned my lesson," I said primly.

"And so have I," Adam said with a serious expression. "Looks mean nothing to me either. I can hang out with any hideous old troll now and not mind."

I kicked him. He grabbed my foot.

"OK, you two." Will held up his hands. "I'm only just adjusting to the new arrangements in the love department. I think it's only fair that you keep your relationship to yourselves when Georgia and I are around. Agreed?"

Adam and I looked at each other. "Agreed."

Will sighed. "Clearly the mountain air has caused Adam to completely lose his mind and *definitely* his eyesight if he finds *Emma* attractive. It must be snow-blindness. I don't know why you didn't get together in the first place and save yourselves a lot of hassle."

"Emma wanted her Austrian dream boy," Georgia explained. "You said nothing else would do, didn't you?"

"Aaaargh! Don't remind me," I wailed, putting my face in my hands. "What was I thinking?"

"What were you thinking indeed?" Adam sighed, brushing a strand of hair out of my face.

"OK, now *what* did I just say?" Will raised his hands in desperation.

The rest of the day was perfect. Josie didn't want to come to the village with us, for a start. In fact, she'd been in a bit of a mood since she got up, banging around noisily in the kitchen, even though we had cleared away all our breakfast things. And she seemed to be positively *avoiding* Dad. We all tramped down to the village and bundled into the candlelit church to listen to carols, and then we walked all the way round the lake.

"Isn't this lovely?" Georgia sighed happily.

"Wonderful," I agreed, watching Nina chase Adam and Will along the path, a snowball clutched in her gloved hand.

"This Christmas has been brilliant, Georgia.

The best ever! And so much of that is because of you. I'm sorry I was such a self-centred idiot at the beginning."

"But it all worked out brilliantly in the end," Georgia smiled. "Everyone had a good time. Even your Dad's accident didn't seem to stop him enjoying himself. Though Josie was in a mood this morning, wasn't she? What was the matter with her? I think she's looking forward to us all going home."

But I didn't want to think about going home. Not today.

A snowball suddenly smashed against my shoulder. Ambush! We were off, running through the trees after a giggling Will, Adam and Nina.

After a huge lunch back at the chalet we left the grown-ups collapsed on the sofas being tortured by Nina with her Pop Princess microphone, and met up with Franz, Dizzy, Bella, Hamish and Ian to go sledging.

"You won't believe the latest..." Bella gasped, as we climbed up the hill. "Guess who's crazy about Janine?"

"Shrek?" Adam offered. I jabbed him with my elbow.

"No, silly," Bella cried. "Gordon! He asked her out last night and she said yes!"

"And that's not all. Lenka is now dating the Spanish girl's brother."

"She'd better brush up on her clapping then," Will grumbled.

"Oh, come on, Will, you'll get over it." Dizzy grinned.

But Will wasn't listening. He was staring at a tall blonde girl standing at the top of the slope in front of us.

"Will...?" Dizzy frowned.

He turned round and looked at us all. "What?"

"*Will...*" I said. "You are a very bad person. Can't you just stop chasing the girls for one minute!" And then we all jumped on him and rolled him in the snow.

At the end of the day I stood in the hall with Adam under the mistletoe that Mr Temple had hung up.

"That was a brilliant day," he whispered. "Best Christmas ever."

I pushed my hand through his thick hair.

"I can't believe I didn't see it was you all along."

"Neither can I really, but there you go. I have

added 'Not very self aware' to your list."

I gave him a shove. "Why did it have to be *you*? You're horrible to me."

"Why did it have to be *you*? Lenka was *so* much nicer to me. I don't understand…"

"You don't understand what?"

"I don't understand why I feel the need to be near you all the time."

He moved closer.

"Mum! Mum!" A piercing shriek echoed through the chalet as Nina, tottering in a pair of glittery heels, yelled back into the sitting room. "They have to get married now! Adam and Emma are KISSING!"

"So what did you learn from your holiday adventures?"

Natalie was perched on a chair next to my bed.

I lay back and stared at the photo of Adam I'd stuck to the wall.

"I learned, Natalie, that it's very hard to work out why some people click and some don't. And when you don't click you have to realize that it doesn't mean it's because you're boring, or not good-looking or funny enough; it's just one of those things. But when you *do*, it's the best feeling in the whole wide world."

"So are you over Sam Harrison then?" Parisa asked, scrolling through my holiday photos on the computer.

"Completely," I sighed.

"And are you going to see this Adam who, I have to say, is pretty gorgeous," Parisa observed, "again?"

"Yes. Yes. Yes. He's coming up with his family in a few weeks for Dad's engagement party."

"Oh my God," cried Parisa. "I'd forgotten about that.

I couldn't believe the news when I read your text. How do you feel about another woman coming to live in your house?"

I filled them in on all the gory details, starting with the difficult conversation we had had with Dad on the day we got back from Austria.

As soon as we'd got home, he had sat us both down in the kitchen, looking agitated.

"I've got something important to say to you both, and I don't want you to say anything until I've finished." Will and I had stared at each other. I had seen the way Dad had looked when Mr and Mrs Temple kissed on Christmas Day. A shadow of sadness had crossed his face and I know that Will had seen it too. It had made us both feel guilty.

When we had said goodbye, Mrs Temple hugged me and said, "Look after your dad, Emma, and remember, when people meet someone special, you shouldn't stand in their way."

It seemed that Will and I were going to have to admit defeat. It was the only thing to do. It didn't mean we weren't miserable about it though.

Dad had put on a serious face. "I think you two

realize that I've become very fond of someone recently."

We kept silent and he went on. "More than fond, actually. I'm aware from our conversation in the sleigh that day that you don't think it's a good idea and that you don't think I know what I'm doing, but I'm a grown man and I can assure you that I think what I'm doing is absolutely right."

"Is she going to come and live here then?" Will murmured. "With us?"

"Yes, she is, Will, and I hope that you'll try and make her very welcome. I would have thought you'd be pleased."

"Pleased!" I cried, all ideas of keeping quiet flying out of the window. "*Pleased!* She's a hard-faced control freak wannabe writer, who's going to file our *souls* away … *and* she wears horrible eye make-up and cheap fishnet tights—"

"I've never worn a pair of fishnet tights in my life!"

We looked round to see Rosie standing in the doorway. It was great to see her familiar smiling face.

"Not you, Rosie!" I shrieked, jumping up to give her a hug. "This awful woman who's coming to live with us."

Rosie looked enquiringly at Dad.

"I thought that awful woman was *me*," she said. "So tell me, who's this lady in fishnet tights then?"

Will and I were both staring at Dad. He was staring back, his hands clapped over his cheeks.

"Josie?!" he shouted at us. "Josie?!" He burst out laughing. "Are you two mad or what? Oh come on – Josie!" He began to pace around the kitchen table. "She's half my age, and everything else you said just then, Emma. I'll admit she took very good care of me and I'll admit that, yes, she may have had a slight crush on me ... she even made a bit of a move on me on the night of the party, which gave me a bit of a surprise. I told her about Rosie pretty sharpish. Really you two ... *Josie!*"

"You read her book," I protested.

"Yes, I did read her book and it was awful. She may be neat and tidy, but she's no writer."

Dad went over to Rosie and put his arms round her. "No, this, *this* is the woman I was talking about. Does that make things any better at all?"

Will and I leaped around the kitchen, pulling Rosie with us. "By a million miles!" I yelled.

"Ah, that's so sweet!" said Natalie.

"I can't wait for the party," added Parisa. "Especially if we'll get to meet the gorgeous Adam."

"Oh, and guess what – Sam Harrison's asked Chanelle Carter out!" said Natalie.

"Well, all I can say is that she better take her whistle and some half-time oranges!"

Natalie laughed. "So you found out that being funny, interesting and able to talk about anything that comes into your head, no matter what, is a good thing in a relationship?"

"I did," I replied, remembering my last night in Austria.

We had been walking in the woods, returning from a meal in the village and the others had gone on ahead.

"So when did you realize that you liked me?" I had asked Adam.

"About half a second after you first walked into the chalet. You were so pretty. I couldn't believe I was going to get to spend two weeks under the same roof as you."

I'd stopped dead. "Wow, Adam. That was a really nice thing to say."

He'd clutched my coat and drawn me towards him.

"Good. You can cross out 'Never gives a compliment' in your practice date notebook now."

"Hmm… I might just wait until I've received a few more before I do that," I'd teased.

He'd pulled me closer. "So, tell me, what's my score?"

I'd looked up, straight into his grey eyes. "Don't let this go to your head, but I reckon you're ten out of ten."

He'd looked pleased with himself. "Wow, even in the kissing category? Are you sure you shouldn't check that out again?"

"Do you think I'd better?" I'd asked, our lips almost touching.

"I do."

And as we'd kissed I knew I'd found the boy I'd been dreaming about for so long.